Natalie & Antonella
in Rome

Natalie & Antonella in Rome

G. D. SPILSBURY

Bergamot Books
www.bergamotbooks.com
Please contact Bergamot Books for permission to copy or use material from the book.

Designed by Leslie Dickersin
Cover design by Nathan Dickersin-Prokopp

FRONTISPIECE: Sarcophagus lid depicting Larth Tetnies and Thanchvil Tarnai (late 4th–early 3rd century BC). Photo © Museum of Fine Arts, Boston.

ISBN 978-1-7354275-9-1
PRINTED IN THE UNITED STATES

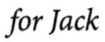

for Jack

The course of true love never did run smooth.

WILLIAM SHAKESPEARE

Overture
(1995)

Rome's summer heat stifled the city. Luckily the wedding reception took place on a high hill, where an imperial palace crowned the summit. It was somewhat cooler up there with acres of undulating nature embellished with relics from a once fantastical and romantic past. But maintaining the property, along with its lifestyle, had become financially impossible for the twentieth-century heirs, and they had sold it to the Italian state. The palace then became a venue for events and the vast grounds a public park.

It was a perfect night—the kind Rome was known for, its mystery and magic permeating the air. Stars twinkled over the palace's grand terrace where guests gathered, their voices lilting, their laughter tinkling into the night's eternal vault. Tall pine trees with bushy tops dotted the land beyond the terrace like dark sentries guarding the grounds. Most of the guests were the bride and groom's friends from the

"Farnesina"—the foreign ministry's nickname. They clustered in groups, nibbled from platters of food, or sat at tables ringing the terrace. Antonella Rosini and Natalie Edwards, close friends at the ministry, chatted with one another at one of the tables. Both were beautiful women in different ways— Natalie, in her seventies, was glamorous with a platinum blonde coiffure and an immaculate summer suit garnished with gold jewelry. Antonella, forty years younger, had a mane of coppery curls and wore a silk dress that clung to her slender figure.

"I know I'm always complaining, but I'm so sick of the way we do business here—and the government's unending red tape," Natalie said in her low, assured voice as she took a sip of her wine, her manicured fingers with red tips extended.

"It's more universal than you think," Antonella said.

"I disagree. Other countries do much better. It's ingrained in our behavior to postpone work and then do the job at the last minute—and slapdash."

"But maybe that's what gives us a corner on the market in art—maybe postponing gives us the space we need to create beauty."

"No, we like to create food and enjoy eating more than working. I've spent the entire year waiting for my neighbor to buy my apartment."

"Why don't you find another buyer?"

"Because it's not so easy—not if I want to rent back."

Antonella nodded sympathetically. She had heard Natalie's apartment story many a time: If Natalie sold her apartment on the open market, she wouldn't have enough equity to rent even a studio in her fashionable Parioli neighborhood. How could she possibly face her friends if she had to live in one of those horrible concrete monstrosities that coated Rome's outskirts? But if she sold her pad to her neighbor at a good discount, he was only too happy to rent it back to her for her remaining years.

"Believe me, surviving on an Italian pension is a daily nightmare," Natalie continued. "It's not like I'm going to inherit a fortune from my father."

"If you're talking about me, I don't count on anything from Rosini. His business is based on trends. And besides, the Mafia has found him."

"Ha! Proof of his success! Let's just hope he has good lawyers—if there's still a shred of law left in this country." Natalie paused and then chuckled. "He could always put a voodoo spell on them, or better yet, send them a custom-brewed potion that puts an end to their nefarious ambitions."

Antonella laughed. Her father, Filippo Rosini, was a tall, bearded alchemist of healing potions. He and Antonella's mother, Jenny Lowe, a Californian, lived in a remote area of Umbria, where Rosini produced organic herbal remedies for every malady known to man. Over the years, his experiments and inventions—based on a lifetime of studying ancient texts—had grown into a homeopathic empire. Jenny, a former yoga and Reiki teacher, had devoted herself to his career. The family's eighteenth-century villa in the middle of nowhere was far from any schools, so various American, French, and Italian tutors had come to live with them over the years of Antonella's childhood. At age twelve, she had been sent to an American boarding school in Rome and only came home for vacations. In retrospect, Antonella felt she had grown up completely unknown to her parents.

Suddenly, a good-looking man with tousled blond hair and ordinary attire stopped at their table—he was the wedding photographer. One hand held his camera and the other an equipment bag, which he dropped to the ground while smiling at them. "Hey ladies, could you move a little closer for a couple of shots?" His voice was deep and sexy as he cast a special look at Antonella. He was just the kind of man women felt instant attraction to, Antonella thought, leaning closer to Natalie for the shot. It was attraction based on physical qualities—the man's height, body build, and masculine aura, an essence that pulsed from him.

"Now say cheese," he said in his gruff but pleasant voice.

"You're American," Antonella said, as her lips held their pose for "cheese."

"Yup. Wyoming—where the buffalo roam. But I left there long ago."

"For here?"

"Nope, New York first—film school—then Italy. I had an internship here with an Italian camera crew."

"And you stayed," Natalie said.

"Because you met someone," Antonella said with a knowing smile.

"Yup. She was an extra on the same film. But we didn't last too long, though we have a son. I'm Gene Wilson, by the way." He extended his right hand first to Antonella. "I heard you two speaking English—American English."

"Yeah, we do that a lot," Antonella said. "We're inter-preters and mix up our languages. Plus, I'm half American—Antonella Rosini." She let go of his hand. "And this is my friend, Natalie Edwards, she's Polish-Bulgarian."

"And formerly married to an American," Natalie said, shaking Gene's hand. "Italian was my last language."

Gene lingered by their table, showing obvious interest in Antonella. And though she usually wore a protective armor around men she didn't know, Gene's physique was a magnet. Besides, this was a wedding, everyone was a friend.

"So, are you still a cameraman or did you switch to pho-tography?" she asked.

"Weddings are just my sideline. Films are hard to get. And since you asked, or sort of asked, my main interest is writing—screenplays. Unfortunately, no takers yet."

At that moment, the foreign ministry's new secretary for Balkan affairs—a Bulgarian—joined their table, sliding into the chair next to Natalie. He was young, dark haired, and quite handsome. Natalie's ice-blue eyes lit up. "Mr. Pavlov!" she said. "At last we meet!"

"Yes, I've been waiting—forever it seems—to meet you, Signora Edwards," the young man said, kissing her hand.

"And it shouldn't take a wedding to bring colleagues, espe-cially kinsmen, together. I have no doubt our families knew each other back in the day, before that horrible war changed everything."

"I'm sure they did, Varna's small," he said, meaning its class divisions. "I've been wanting to tell you about my cousin who's making a film about your uncle, Anton Leviev. No one back home knows he had a niece here in Italy—it's a big discovery."

"Good to know I'm a big discovery," Natalie said.

"We're curious to know if you settled here because of him."

"No, not exactly. It was a series of escapes," Natalie said.

Antonella got up to chat more with Gene, as she had already heard Natalie's story many times before. Nevertheless, the older woman's purring voice followed her like a well-rehearsed recording. "I was four months old when the Red Army stormed Kiev, slaughtering the aristocrats, which included my father's Polish family—the Jablonskis."

"And what about you, Antonella, how did you end up in Rome?" Gene asked with flirtatious blue eyes. "And wait, I want to get a few shots of you for the bride and groom." He touched her shoulder, then her chin to adjust her pose before stepping back to rapidly snap pictures. Antonella held the pose, aware of tingling inside from Gene's light touch.

"Work," Antonella answered him. "First New York, straight out of grad school, then Brussels, and now Rome—the ministry. Probably my last stop."

"Bodes well for me," Gene joked.

Antonella smiled but didn't answer, while Natalie's voice purred continuously from the table.

"Uncle Anton was my mother's brother. He traveled widely studying art. In India he was good friends with Tagore. I have his painting of Tagore. Eventually, he settled in Florence."

"And did you connect with him there?" Mr. Pavlov asked.

"Yes, my mother and I lived with him for seven years, until I was ten. He taught me to draw and paint. I was like a daughter to him. But my mother, poor thing, couldn't get along with anyone, not even her brother. So we moved to Sofia where my mother—who was a great beauty—married one of the king's advisers. We lived there until the end of the Second World War."

To show he was doing his job, Gene began snapping pictures of guests at the neighboring tables while continuing to talk to Antonella. He told her some of the films he had worked on, but she hadn't seen any. When she asked where he lived, he made a disgusted face—"Way up the Cassia—god-awful traffic—but affordable," he said. Then he dug in his camera bag and pulled out a dirty business card. "Here—let's stay in touch, meet for coffee sometime?"

Antonella nodded and took his card, glad he was the one to suggest another encounter. She fished in her purse for her card and held it out—crisp and clean, the opposite of his. They smiled at each other, business successfully concluded. Gene picked up his bag and headed off for more picture taking. Antonella sat back down and let her gaze follow his broad back and long legs as he moved through the guests and tables, his manly profile a definite enticement.

Natalie had kept an eye on Antonella while delivering her early history to Mr. Pavlov. It was the first time she had seen Antonella show attraction to a man. Weddings had a way of stirring romance. And Natalie was dying for Antonella to find a husband and have children. Her young friend was thirty-five, with her biological clock ticking down. Natalie didn't want Antonella to miss out on having children the way she had. Her marriage to Woody had ended in divorce after a few volatile years, and she had never remarried.

Never interrupting the flow of her story while her thoughts wandered to Antonella, Natalie said to Mr. Pavlov, "When the Russians stormed our family's home in 1919, my mother and I were upstairs in the nursery. She heard the terrible screaming as the murders took place in the parlor. She managed to escape from a window with me in her arms."

Mr. Pavlov shook his head incredulously. "I'm so sorry…"

"Well, obviously, I was told all this later—though I'm sure the trauma entered my psyche for life. We hid, we kept moving from dark barns and cellars—friends helped us, but never for long, for that would have put their lives in danger. Weeks, maybe months, passed like that—hungry, dirty, living in terror. Finally, word reached Uncle Anton in Florence, and he found a way to cross borders and find us. He took us to my grandparents in Varna. We traveled on trains carrying cargo and animals. There was no coal, and whenever the train ran out of fuel, the men jumped off and collected sticks or scraps of wood so we could continue on."

"Amazing, signora! Back home, no one knows this story. My cousin will want to interview you for the film, if you're willing. And do you have any of Anton's art? Or photographs?"

"I have both. And I'd be delighted to help your cousin with his film—let's talk more next week." She turned to Antonella on her other side. "You're back, and with a future beau, I see."

Antonella made a face as if accustomed to Natalie's boyfriend prodding.

Mr. Pavlov got up and extended his hand. "I'm so happy we finally met, signora."

"And so am I, Mr. Pavlov. We'll continue next week. I'm at the ministry most days—officially retired but still helping out."

Mr. Pavlov kissed her hand, then grinned. "I still need to hear how you ended up in Rome."

"The suspense will do you good. But here's a hint—it was our second great escape from the Communists." She flashed her glamorous smile at him, and he bowed once more to kiss her hand fondly before leaving.

At that moment, the band across the terrace struck up its first song. The lead singer put his lips to the mic and welcomed the bride and groom to lead the opening dance.

Antonella got up, "Something to eat?" she asked Natalie.

"No thanks, my dear, I'm quite content just sitting here."

Antonella went off to peruse the buffet tables laden with appetizers and other courses, though desserts had not yet arrived. Their display of irresistible delicacies would accompany the wedding cake in a supporting role, luckily on a separate table.

The central terrace soon filled up as couples joined the bride and groom for dancing. Too bad Gene was working, Antonella thought, imagining his bearlike arms coming into contact with her for a dance. She couldn't find him through the moving crowd and hoped they'd bump into each other again—could he possibly take a short break and dance with her? Letting out a wistful sigh, she forced herself to focus on the array of tantalizing appetizers and chose a crispy rice ball—a *suppli*—made small enough to pop whole in her mouth, but large enough to completely fill it. Of course, it was just then—as soon as she had popped the whole ball into her mouth—that a pleasant voice behind her said, "Care to dance?"

She whirled around covering her mouth and found herself face-to-face with a handsome man of medium height, whose brown eyes with dark lashes smiled directly into hers. His rather tender lips turned up with the same hopeful lift of his eyebrows—was she free to dance? She noticed his trim, compact shape, every part in proportion. He wore short sleeves and dress pants—no jacket or tie—probably left behind over a chair somewhere.

"So sorry," she mumbled, trying to swallow.

"Don't worry, I caught you at a bad moment. But those *suppli* are great—I had a few myself. How about a dance?—after you swallow."

His unaffected friendliness reassured her and she nodded. He lightly touched her arm and guided her to the middle of the busy dance area. It was then and there that the real magic of the starlit wedding night began for Antonella—and for Lawrence. They danced the entire set, their bodies moving easily, gracefully together and with each song growing ever more accustomed to the other's body. They talked whenever their heads came together and also between songs. He was Lawrence Gaspari, a doctor, thirty-seven, and living in Rome's upscale Prati neighborhood across the Tiber from her own place in Monti. He told her he loved dancing, and he hummed or sang along to all the band's songs. Antonella basked in his natural control of her movements, dipping and twirling her, thrusting her away from him only to pull her back with a knock against his chest, always with his friendly smile and deep-set eyes so close.

Once in a while, Antonella noticed Gene taking pictures and glancing at them with a frown, as if jealous of a rival. But it was true, Antonella thought, Lawrence was a rival, and she would give him her number before she left the party. That meant that both men would be calling her, and what would she do then? Did she intend to see both? Get involved with both?

Lawrence spun her so that she glimpsed Natalie, still seated at the table though no longer alone. The ministry's much-loved Ambassador de Berto had joined her and the two were chin-wagging away, as if recalling old times in their long careers.

By the time the band took its break, Antonella knew Lawrence's whole body and wanted it, and he knew hers and wanted it. Why, she wondered, had she met two men who sent electricity through her on the same night? And in different ways—Gene's sexy brawn and Lawrence's agile sensuality. Especially given her barriers to men who came on to her too fast, as if only interested in sex. And yet, that's what was happening to her—an instinctive, physical attraction. But was it only physical? Did the invisible neurotransmitters of lust also intuit something deeper about certain people—what was good or compatible on an inner level? All she knew was that she and Lawrence had become closer in spirit with each dance, as if dancing were a communication like talking, as if body language had united them in some uncanny way when they had begun as total strangers.

As the last song began—and it was a slow one—

Lawrence held out his arms and Antonella moved into them. He pressed his head lightly to hers, and she closed her eyes to better feel his pliant body under his summer clothes. Their hands changed positions, touching, exploring politely. With her cheek on his neck, she drew in his damp, sweet smell like an aphrodisiac and longed to leave the party and go straight to his place or hers to make love. She regretted hearing the band's climatic drum roll ending the song. She felt Lawrence's lips press into her dense curls—a kiss of thanks, a kiss of familiarity and promise. They came apart and stared at each other with wonder in their eyes and smiles, their future already determined but as yet unknown.

Rocca del Cielo

The working breakfast at the Farnesina wrapped up. The handsomely groomed American delegation shook hands warmly with their Italian counterparts from the ministry and the business community. Their weeklong negotiations had ended favorably. Antonella also received warm handshakes for her interpretation, along with those typical glances of men that ran over her body. Her gracious smile never wavered at this age-old patriarchal treatment of women, even though she hated it. She didn't linger for chitchat but headed out, her mind on the weekend ahead. She and Natalie had planned a getaway to the Tuscan coast long before the impromptu breakfast for the Americans had been scheduled. Natalie was now waiting for her in the employees' café.

Antonella's dress shoes tapped like percussion as she crossed the ministry's big marble lobby. Several corridors later, she could hear lively voices in the distance, as if a big party were in full swing. She smiled to herself—it was the employees' café. All kinds of conversation took place there, from complaints about work and bosses, to ideas for Sunday outings, to flirting and nailing a date. Her fellow countrymen (and women) loved to socialize. They loved to be near beautiful food while they chatted away, and in the morning, the bar's glass case displayed mounds of mouthwatering pastries, their surfaces glistening with glaze, jam, or powdered sugar. At lunchtime, trays of succulent sandwiches replaced the morning fare. If someone wanted a more substantial meal—pasta or second courses—the cafeteria offered a daily menu.

Antonella entered the crowded bar. Coworkers stood at the counter or sat at marble-top tables, everyone talking as if time didn't exist. She waved to Natalie at a table across the room. She was always easy to spot with her globe of platinum hair.

Natalie pushed back her chair to rise, noticing how men at the bar turned to eye Antonella with that full-body appraisal Natalie knew so well—women as sex objects instead of intelligent human beings. But Antonella's generation had it better than hers—they could demand respect and equal rights, even if they didn't get them. And of course, she acknowledged that women also eyed attractive men, herself included, but the scales and stakes were drastically uneven. For one, women didn't corner, coerce, or force sex on men. More important, they valued men's character more than their sex appeal.

"Natalie!" Ambassador de Berto's voice called out as he

came into the bar, guiding the elbow of a heavyset man in a shiny black suit. Antonella joined their step to meet Natalie in the middle of the room.

"Natalie, I'd like you to meet Gianni Garella, our aircraft coordinator. We're so fortunate to have his expertise." He bowed lightly to Garella, who bowed back. "And this is Signora Edwards, our most senior and valued interpreter, besides being a much sought-after painter." Back to Natalie he said, "Signor Garella hopes you'll paint his family."

Natalie, looking perfectly petite in a rose suit, offered her hand with shining gold bracelets and received Garella's formal kiss just above her fingers.

"I'm so honored to make your acquaintance, signora, not only because of your distinguished career for Italy, but also for your gifts as a painter—I happened to see your portrait of Pope John Paul II."

Natalie's dazzling smile never diminished. "Oh, yes, done so long ago but still one of my favorites. I'd be delighted to paint your family, Signor Garella, but let's confer next week. I'm just leaving for the weekend with my friend." She nodded at Antonella and then opened her purse for her business card.

"Thank you, signora, I'll call you next week," Garella said, taking her card and at the same time bowing with another simulated kiss above her hand.

Ambassador de Berto, pleased with the outcome of his mission, kissed Natalie on both cheeks. "Thank you, my dear, I hope this works out." He then touched Garella's elbow to lead him to the bar for the essential caffè.

"We're off," Antonella said.

"Yes, it's now or never—the entire ministry's here—for the day."

They chuckled and headed briskly for the door before anyone else could detain them.

At last they were on the road and beyond the city limits, Antonella at the wheel of her blue Fiat Panda. It was late morning, the sun bright in a pure azure sky, October's shadows hard on roughly furrowed farmland belonging to peeling stucco houses, red and beige.

"I so needed this escape, Toni," Natalie said, gazing out the window. "Thank you so much for planning it."

"I need it too, work was insane this week—the Americans are way too focused."

"There's nothing like the Americans, I know, I was married to one."

"And my mother was the entrepreneur for my father's genius."

"I see a little of both in you."

"I see only myself in me."

"Well, of course, that's the best outcome," Natalie said.

It was almost lunchtime when they reached Rocca del Cielo's high hill and took the switchback road to its summit. The medieval town was beautiful, its stone structures overlooking an infinite expanse of sea that seemed to hold a phantom past of seafaring Greeks and Romans—Virgil, Cleopatra, Ovid, and others from all the lost civilizations whose essences and myths sparkled on waves. Rocca's old villas, hotels, and humbler homes rose to the sky from its steep, terraced slope, at the bottom of which lay a small harbor with fishing boats that rocked against their moorings. A sleek foreign yacht looked incongruous among them, like a giant white insect. A beach was down there too, but barely visible from the hilltop's height.

Two liveried men from the hotel's entrance helped the women from their car, whisked their luggage to a porter, and then drove the Panda away to another location, for the old hill town with narrow, cobbled streets did not allow cars. The women felt excitement as their eyes took in the picturesque beauty surrounding them—ancient arches, winding stone streets, and doorsteps with potted plants and lazing cats—all of which beckoned them to explore. In early October it was warm and nature still bloomed. Purple bougainvillea coated entire walls, and in the hotel's small, half-moon courtyard giant urns overflowed with red geranium vines that trailed the ground like long peacock feathers in the breeze. Lemon trees added bright yellow splotches, and underfoot lay a mosaic of small stones polished smooth by time.

"This is nice," Natalie purred.

"Mmm," Antonella agreed.

Inside was a realm of elegance—shining marble, tile, wood, and glass. Baroque-style furniture reflected in gigantic, gilded mirrors. Natalie appraised the decor with satisfaction, noting in particular the open French doors to a sun-drenched terrace with lounge chairs and scattered tables—her preferred place to park for the weekend. On the opposite side of the lobby, through another set of French doors, was the dining room, its regal decor like a painting whose furnishings could never be disturbed.

"Perfect," Natalie said.

"Picked just for you," Antonella said, "with the ministry's discount, of course."

"Thank you, you know my taste."

They checked in at the reception desk. The handsome young clerk, dressed impeccably in a blue suit, was more than happy to attend to Antonella and barely glanced at Natalie. As he handed Antonella their key cards, he smiled solicitously and said, "Let me know if there's anything I can help you with, and your mother."

"My friend," Antonella said.

"I don't need any help, thank you," Natalie snapped.

"Of course not, signora, my sincere apologies."

"We'd like to go to the beach—what's the best way down?" Antonella asked.

"Ah—our beach!" he said, taking one of the hotel's tourist maps and marking it with a pen. "You should take the steps down—they're direct and picturesque." He circled them and then looked up with a fresh smile for Antonella. "If you like, I can show you."

"Oh, no, we're fine on our own. But thanks."

Natalie watched the exchange and how Antonella handled it so pleasantly. The clerk couldn't possibly feel rejected, even though he was. In her own day, women had felt guilty for saying no to a man's advances, as if they were wrong to deny a man his rights. And how many times had she seen women support staff lose their jobs for saying no? But the problem still existed. Many men still believed any woman they took on a date, or employed, or did some favor for, owed them sex. It was atrocious.

"Be sure to visit the eleventh-century church—you'll see a sign for it at the rotary, where the steps end. The frescoes have been restored—it's a World Heritage Site," the clerk was telling Antonella, still hoping to impress her. "Here, I've marked everything on the map."

"Thanks! We'll be sure to see the church," Antonella said, softening the way Natalie snatched the map from the clerk's fingers.

They took the elevator to their room on the second floor. It was spacious and high-ceilinged with two double beds, a modern bathroom that undoubtedly had problems, and a small balcony overlooking an inner courtyard that was beautifully planted and peaceful. They settled in, unpacking their few belongings and eating a light lunch delivered by room service.

"And now for our walk," Antonella said, getting up and changing into casual capris and sandals for the beach.

"I'll wear what I have on," Natalie said, smoothing the A-line skirt of her rose suit. "But I guess I'll have to wear these." She sat on the edge of her bed to put on sneakers, but stylish ones with gold spangles and hot-pink laces. "My mother would die if she saw me wearing these—so 'unladylike.' You know, today's her birthday."

"I didn't know."

"She'd be ninety-seven."

"A good reason to celebrate our weekend."

"I'm not sure I'd ever celebrate anything about my mother. She was nasty, always finding fault with everyone—how we looked, how we behaved. Did I ever tell you my birthday story?"

"I don't think so."

"Every year on my birthday, she'd sit me down as if I were being punished and shake her finger in my face: 'This is actually my anniversary, Natalie—the anniversary of my terrible suffering because of you, giving birth to you!'"

"Jeez, that's horrible…"

"I had to hear that before she'd let me open my presents. When I got old enough, I told her to stop, I couldn't take it anymore. But now, probably because of my age, I think I'd put up with her rather than be alone. You see, we survived wars together, people trying to murder us. We kept each other going. And ultimately, she was my mother, by nature my shield, and now I have no protection."

"You have me!"

"Thank you, *tesoro*, I appreciate it, and believe me, I'm grateful for our friendship. I don't know anyone else I can confide in, the way I can with you."

"Same goes for me."

"Even so, there's something uncanny about family, the blood bond, that can't be explained. It's an innate connection between humans."

Natalie sighed and got up from the bed, stamping her twinkling sneakers a few times. She picked up her sketchpad and pastels that had been beside her on the bed and put them on the dresser, meeting Antonella's eyes in the mirror above it.

"What're you going to sketch here? People? Cats?" Antonella asked.

"Hard to say. I love faces the most, seeing what's inside a person—for better or worse. But those lemon trees in the courtyard—they really grabbed me." She smiled at Antonella's reflection. "Maybe I'll sketch you. I've been dying to. I especially love your face when it's turned three-quarters away from me."

She reached up and turned Antonella's head to the desired position. "*Ecco*—you're straight from Botticelli's brush—his Venus—down to the color of your gold-brown eyes. I always wonder, is beauty a blessing or a curse?"

"The real question is: would you forfeit it?"

"No."

They headed out, Natalie opening her pocketbook to be sure she had everything she might need for the beach. She saw Woody's notecard and pulled it out as the elevator doors opened for them. "I got this yesterday," she said, showing the card to Antonella.

"Oh?—a new suitor?"

"Hmm, you might say so. Or an old one—Woody. He's back in Rome and sent me this card along with flowers. He wants to have lunch next week."

"Wow—that's big news … Woody. I wonder what this means?"

"Nothing. It means nothing, but I'm glad he's here. I'm glad we don't have anger anymore—just friendly feelings.

That's what old age does—either from wisdom or loss of memory."

Antonella laughed. "So, when do I get to meet him?"

"Let us get reacquainted first. We haven't seen each other since the 1950s."

"You mean you never went to New York? Not even for work?"

"Never. And if he came to Rome, he didn't tell me. But we did write letters now and then. A few calls, mainly about money. We stayed in touch, cordially."

Antonella smiled. "Looks like you have a busy week ahead, Nat—the guy who wants portraits, the Bulgarian film about your uncle, and now Woody."

"The last the most important."

"I'll say. Gee, what if…?" her voice trailed off.

Natalie stepped out of the elevator before the doors had fully finished opening, Antonella's words reverberating in her ears and causing anxiety: *What if*? Exactly what she had been thinking since Woody's return—*what if*? What if they got together again? But no, Woody undoubtedly still ate dinner at six and hated the Italian way of socializing at cafés between five and seven p.m., which was her favorite part of the day— *chiacchiericcio*—carefree chitchat with friends, along with an espresso or an aperitif, accompanied by a delicious tidbit, sweet or savory depending on one's choice of beverage. No, she couldn't share his life, and he couldn't share hers. They had fought like cats and dogs when under the same roof. Though, of course, Donka had been a factor, always flinging her venom at both of them in the small apartment they shared after the war. Now Woody was back and Donka was dead. Had he returned for her? To finish their lives together? *Oh Dio, what if*?

Natalie paused at the open terrace doors for a glimpse of the leisure ladies in scant clothing sunbathing on lounge chairs. White turbans wrapped their heads, and cigarettes dangled from their languid fingers. How she would love to join them instead of taking a walk. She would sit at one of the tables and enjoy October's clear light and fragrant air—the hilltop's peace and quiet. She would sketch the ladies or read the newspaper. Better yet, she would answer Woody's card while sipping a scotch. But she couldn't face disappointing Antonella, who was so keen on taking the steps to the beach. It was at times like this that their age difference showed— Natalie less energetic than in her younger years, now more inclined to sit, observe, converse, or reflect. Antonella was still driven by libido's energy, curiosity, and willingness to take risks. And besides, now she had crushes on two men at the same time—the ones she had met at the August wedding. Love always produced adrenaline and physical radiance.

Each lost in her own thoughts, they passed through the city's gate and soon arrived at the steps to the beach. A most incredible sea view lay before their eyes. But Natalie could not appreciate it. All she could see was the steps, steps descending a cliffside at a 45-degree angle. Steps of ancient vintage and handwrought construction—rough and irregular—surrounded by terraced gardens and vineyards in their withered, tangled, autumnal state—the picturesque part. How was she going to manage those steps with her bad back and knees?

Just then the hotel clerk came around the same corner. "Oh ladies!" he said cheerfully, "I see you found the steps!"

"Indeed we did, and I see they're much too much for my bad back and knees. I'm so sorry, Toni, I'll have to take a taxi down and meet you there," Natalie said, using Antonella's nickname.

The clerk instantly blew a shrill whistle through his thumb and forefinger, and a taxi came around the same corner as if everything had been prearranged. With a big smile, the clerk opened the back door for Natalie, who was forced to grudgingly thank him. To his surprise, Antonella got right in after Natalie, tossing back her own thanks. Natalie chuckled, and the cab drove away.

After numerous and dizzying switchbacks down the cliffside road, they reached the bottom with a rotary and paths leading off of it. The taxi driver let them out next to the beach path. Antonella wasted no time kicking off her sandals and skipping through the soft, lumpy sand toward the beach. Natalie followed, watching her and feeling déjà vu for herself at that age, full of exuberance and divine connection to the universe that the ocean and its long expanse of sand evoked. With a faint pulse of her old inspiration, she quickened her step, but by the time she reached the beach, her sneakers were full of sand, and she worried about tearing her only pair of nylons for the trip.

"I'm so sorry, my dear, I should have thought ahead to what a beach walk entails. I'm not dressed for it. And I don't intend to take off my shoes and stockings and go barefoot like you."

"Shall we to go back?"

"Yes, but just me. I want nothing more than for you to enjoy your walk. And I just wish I could enjoy it with you. But no matter. I'll meet you back at the hotel. I'll be on the terrace. And happily so."

"But how're you getting back?"

"Don't worry, the steps are much easier going up than going down."

"I'll go with you, Nat."

"No, I won't allow it. I'm fine on my own. But perhaps I should be worrying about you on this deserted beach—with that rapacious clerk, surely by now spying on us from behind those rocks."

Just then, a gust of wind tore into her starched hairdo. Her hands flew up to hold the sculpted waves in place until the wind died down.

Antonella smiled. She was used to Natalie's concerns, like facing all those class-conscious hotel guests at dinnertime, who would be trying to find grist for their gossip mill—anything about other guests' attire, hair, shoes, or jewelry that could be judged maliciously.

"Okay, I'll see you in an hour or so," Antonella said.

"Thank you for understanding. And please don't worry about me. I'll thoroughly enjoy myself on the terrace."

Antonella flashed a fond smile, and for a moment, Natalie stopped and forgot everything but her young friend's three-quarter face framed against the depthless blue sky, her coppery hair wild in the wind, and her complexion flushed with pure femininity. That was it—that was the portrait

Natalie would paint. And with a surprised flutter of her heart, she realized that what she wanted to capture was actually herself at Antonella's age.

"Don't get into trouble," she said dryly.

"I'll be fine, see you later."

Back on the path to the rotary, with less wind, Natalie stopped for a moment to get out her compact and check her hair and makeup. She applied a fresh coat of red lipstick and then rubbed her lips together. As she put the lipstick back in purse, she again noticed Woody's notecard, and her heart lurched. It was an ache for their past, their love that had ended in anger and blame. He was obviously feeling nostalgic too. They had met in Sofia after the war. He had been a handsome, young Air Force officer with the pro-democracy Allied Control Commission, which the Soviets briefly tolerated after they moved in and took control of Bulgaria. Natalie was working for the American general as a translator and office assistant, and he treated her like an adored pet. Woody secretly loved Natalie, as did many of the young men in their mission and beyond. One day, a Russian aide-de-camp, who also desired Natalie, came to the American headquarters to request her translating services for his general. It was just before the communist situation grew dangerous for both the Americans and the remaining Bulgarian elite. Instead of escorting her to the general's office, the aide took her to his own quarters. He locked the door, fell on his knees, and begged her to love him. He recited Pushkin. When she refused his passionate advances, he went berserk. "You're a spy for the Americans!" he shouted, grabbing a chair and swinging it at her. "We hang people like you! You won't get away with this!"

Right then, someone began banging on the door—
Woody—he had followed them, suspecting trouble. When
he broke through the door, she ran to him, crying in terror.
He held her tight, calming her with gentle words, and she
felt utterly safe. Their courtship began that day. She loved his
courage, authority, and American know-how. She loved his
looks and personality.

When the Communists asserted their rule, panic
struck. Donka's royalist husband was arrested and executed
along with thousands of others. There was no time to plan.
Natalie and her mother grabbed as much as they could carry
from their palatial apartment but essentially lost everything.
The American general organized their escape, and Woody
piloted them to Rome. The general also arranged for Natalie
to work as a translator for the Americans, and six months
later, she and Woody eloped to Florence and married with
Uncle Anton's blessing. Donka, however, was furious about
the match and never let up in her nastiness to Woody. The
three of them lived together in Rome, European style, which
was not American style. Woody had obtained his military
discharge and worked at the American Embassy. The marriage ended in acrimony. Besides all their petty arguing and
cultural clashes, Woody demanded that she choose between
him and her mother. She chose her mother. He simply could
not understand the impossibility of abandoning Donka,
especially given her wretched personality. But for Natalie
their bond had to be honored—they had escaped war and
death together. At times they had scrimped and gone hungry

to survive. Their lives were fused. Even now, with her fear of destitution, Natalie believed she would still choose her narcissistic mother over Woody.

She snapped shut her purse and began to walk around the rotary toward the steps to the hotel. Almost immediately, a young man with quintessential Mediterranean looks came down the road on a squealing Vespa and zipped past her. The obnoxious noise shattered the peaceful setting, and Natalie rebelled inside. She hated scooters and blamed the Italians for having them in such abundance. And the fumes lingered forever, defiling exactly what made the countryside so desirable—pure air. She wanted to hurry back to the hotel, away from this dreadful scooter that had just spun around the circle again to shrill past her in a cloud of sand and exhaust. She couldn't wait to sip a scotch on the terrace while writing Woody a letter venting her annoyance. It excited her that Woody was now living across the Borghese Gardens from her. It was too soon to tell where their reconnection would go, but it seemed Woody had mellowed. And so had she. Now, in her seventies, she often pined for a companion, and more than that, for someone to lean on just a little. Woody had always been stronger that way. She had fought it, but now she wanted it.

As Natalie rounded the rotary, the young man on the scooter drove by again, but this time he slowed as he passed her, turning his head to stare at her from behind his cool-man shades. Her heart instantly pumped in fear. So it was happening to her, the scenario she had always heard about—a thief on a scooter targeting her pocketbook. Why had she even brought it to the beach? Because she didn't trust hotel maids.

The villain drove up the hill, like a fox with a tail—his trail of poisonous gas mocking her. Her thoughts raced hard. She knew he'd be back. Should she hide her purse in the scrub and continue walking? No, he would notice it was gone and easily find it. She could hurry and stuff the money into her bra and hand over the purse. But it was deserted here. He would wrestle her to the ground and stick his hand down there. And worse—that would arouse him and he'd rape her. He wouldn't even care about her age. Men had blind animal instincts. And then he'd have to kill her.

This time, he made a big show of gunning his wimpy motor scooter past her with a look at her, as if he were a prize stud she couldn't resist. "*Cretino!*" she hissed.

In a state of panic, she moved mechanically toward the main road, for help might arrive—a taxi. She was barely breathing and her lungs hurt. Her heart pounded in her throat—she could taste the blood. Now the devil was coming back down the hill, very slowly, the scooter making its hideous whine, as if to torture her about her coming fate. What if she kneed him in the balls and made a run for it. But she had no place to run to. As soon as he recovered, he'd go ballistic and smash her to pieces. She saw an image of herself lying bloodied by the roadside.

The villain parked his scooter on the other side of the rotary. Natalie closed her eyes. The day felt utterly surreal, like the sultry, oppressive atmosphere in *L'Étranger*, when Meursault brutally killed the Arab in a blind psychotic state. Natalie shuddered and tried to hang on to her reason. She looked up, and for the first time noticed a faded, rusted bus-stop sign a few feet to her right. Would a bus be coming? Would there be time to wait for it? How incredible that a bus stop should suddenly look like a human savior, like a policeman. She walked briskly to the sign and stood close to its corroded pole, watching her pursuer from behind her sunglasses. He leaned nonchalantly against the scooter's seat, pelvis thrust out to accentuate the bulge in his pants, where he had sanded away the denim over the fly. He ran a hand over his dark hair, making sure it looked its best. His vanity in such a situation was ludicrous, and she felt like laughing at him, albeit hysterically. She kept her right arm over her pocketbook like a crowbar.

Now the miscreant was looking around, double-checking the peaceful, empty circle—not a soul in sight, only Rocca del Cielo's terraced cliff rising steeply above them. It was that view that showed Natalie another rusting sign, this one yellow for tourism, pointing the way to the eleventh-century church the hotel clerk had recommended they see. Her gold-spangled sneakers stepped in that direction and then hesitated. If he followed her, the church would be even more secluded than this circle and its possibility of new arrivals saving her.

His footsteps crunched over the pebbly road in her direction, and she stared at the ground, refusing to acknowledge him. Then the steps paused—ha!—he was using the approach of all beasts of prey—stealth, she thought, and I won't know until it happens whether I fight back or submit. I'll probably fight back even if he has a knife and kills me.

There was another noise. Natalie looked up. Her assailant

had heard it first, and that was why he had stopped. A car was on the last switchback, approaching the circle. Hope, salvation, rushed over her like a cleansing waterfall. Her knees became jelly. She took hold of the bus stop's pole. But then, new thoughts hurtled through her mind, absurd thoughts, like how could she, a lady, flag down a car? How could she allow herself to look like a lunatic that the people in the car would lock their doors against? Even if they did respond, how could she inconvenience them? In the oily blur of the surreal moment, she watched the car slowly pass around the circle and away from her.

Her voice automatically croaked out as in a nightmare, "Help! Wait!" The car parked by the path to the church. An older man and two women got out, tourists. Natalie nodded faintly, politely, to them, and they nodded back. They hadn't heard her shout—thank God for that! She glanced at the young man. He wasn't moving, just watching. She felt a pang of victory and gave him a smug look. Robbery was now out of the question. His head dropped a bit, but he feigned indifference as he sauntered back to his wheels. Still, he dallied there, and she knew he wanted to see if the newcomers would go up the path to the church, leaving her alone again. She steeled herself to take the action she feared most—bothering the tourists, feeling shame and guilt for herself. In her most dignified manner—regretting her sneakers—she approached the visitors with her well-bred smile.

"Good afternoon, signori. I'm feeling uncomfortable with that young man on the motor scooter. He has followed me here, I think with bad intentions."

That ended it. The young man boarded his scooter and peeled off in a cloud of spiteful dust.

Natalie went on to visit the old church with her saviors, who turned out to be French and retired teachers. She spoke French like a native and rattled on about thieves in Italy. Thieves were just as rampant in Paris, her new friends told her. They toured the church together and discussed its ancient frescoes. They got along so famously that on the drive back to Rocca del Cielo, they agreed to meet for an aperitif before dinner that night.

Later that afternoon, when Antonella returned from the beach, she stopped at the hotel's bar and ordered an iced tea. She could see Natalie through the open terrace door, her head bent over a letter she was writing. The lounging ladies were gone, presumably to bathe and dress for the evening ahead.

The TV over the bar showed a popular program hosted by a white-haired man, his body language and face full of self-importance. His name was Bruno Gallo, and his show featured couples with marital problems. Once a week, he and a guest expert gave couples advice on how to resolve their disagreements. On this day, he sat across from a stunning young woman—tall and svelte, with a square, chiseled face and dark hair to her shoulders. She wore a miniskirt that showed off her shapely legs. She was Donatella Gaspari, a sex and couples therapist frequently quoted in the media for her radical views, or radical to Italy's traditions. Antonella knew her from the news, even before she had met Lawrence, Donatella's older brother. Antonella paused at the bar to watch the show for a few minutes, eager to see how that awful misogynist Bruno, whom she normally boycotted, handled a fearless woman like Donatella, or better, how Donatella handled him. Dismantling the patriarchy was a subject dear to Antonella's heart, and Donatella was a heroine for the movement.

Unsmiling people of all ages sat on bleachers on the program's stage listening to the dialogue. The couple with a marital problem sat side by side on a platform between Donatella and Bruno, as if defendants at their trial. Donatella was speaking to the couple. "Listen, my friends, you have a common situation, and I want you to see—and I mean really get it—how twisted and destructive the behavior is, because until you embody that awareness, the world's patriarchal mentality is just going to continue unabated and wreck relationships like yours. Men—or global society controlled by men—has conditioned women to accept lower-species treatment. All of us—men and women—need to wake up and change." She pointed a finger at the husband, a bulky, well-fed, limited-thinking specimen, and her husky, sexy voice rose a decibel. "You cannot control your wife, Guido. You cannot tell her what to wear, or when and with whom she can go out. Do you know what the extreme of that kind of behavior is?"

The husband shrugged dismissively. Bruno rattled his notes and drew a barely tolerant breath that conveyed the same contempt as Guido's shrug. Donatella ignored their insulting behavior.

"I'll tell you what that extreme is. It's when a judge—a person entrusted with justice for all—throws out an important rape case because the victim—who could have been your wife,

Guido—wore jeans. In other words, she provoked the rape by wearing jeans. How would you feel, how would you react to that kind of 'justice' for your traumatized, violated wife? This exact verdict happened last week!"

"I don't want her wearing certain clothes," the husband muttered.

"But think about it—is it a woman's responsibility to prevent you from committing a felony? That's a patriarchal view, exactly what we need to change. In fact, it's your responsibility—it's all men's responsibility—to respect other human beings on the planet."

Bruno's deep, authoritative voice dove in, "Interesting point, Donatella, though I see we have a long way to go if we want our society to become your utopia."

"Utopia? My utopia, Bruno? Why that's patriarchal too. You're equating social equality, fundamental equal respect, to a mere utopian fantasy. Equality and respect are what's right. Brushing them off as a silly dream is just your male way of protecting your power. It's the response of physically more powerful men from the beginning of known human history."

Antonella gave a thumbs up at the TV. "Way to go, girl! Hope I get to meet you soon!" She took her iced tea and headed for the terrace.

Natalie looked up from her writing. Woody's card lay at her elbow. "Why, darling, you're positively glowing—all windblown and beautiful."

"Thanks, but what about you? Your back? Were the steps okay?"

"French tourists gave me a ride."

"Good!" Antonella sat down. "Are you writing Woody?"

"Yes. His return has brought back a flood of memories."

"I can imagine. It's like a whole new world has opened up."

"It has. Did I ever tell you that because of Italy's laws, I couldn't divorce him, and by the time the laws changed, my fiancé, Count Obertelli, had died of a heart attack?"

"Yes, you told me, and I guess if you had married him, you wouldn't be writing Woody now"

Natalie nodded. "No—I'd be safe, probably a widow by now, living in Paolo's palace overlooking the Colosseum. My mother was counting on that marriage. She couldn't wait to move in and finish her life in the comfort she felt had been stolen from her. The entire second floor would have been hers."

Antonella nodded. She knew the consequences of that lost opportunity. Natalie and her mother had gone on as usual, depending on Natalie's salary, portrait commissions, and social connections. But her official retirement had slowly put the squeeze on them, and then Donka had checked out before the bank situation grew dire.

"Money matters," Natalie said blandly.

"It drives the world."

"And there's never enough of it, is there? Every time we think we've made a small gain in our savings, something else comes up—a broken tooth or some new desire that has to be fulfilled at once."

"Like a weekend at Rocca del Cielo."

"Yes, and all for me, I know," Natalie said with an apologetic look at Antonella.

"Not at all, I like luxury too. Everyone on the planet likes it. Luxury feels safe. And we wouldn't have come without the ministry's discount. Anyway, we agree, social divisions are bad."

"Atrocious!"

"And yet, the world's most beautiful art—the art that uplifts us, heals our souls—exists because of greed, wealth, patronage, and criminality. It's art at the expense of the artists and the masses."

"Most of the time, yes, and again, I'm guilty—my grandparents had serfs and collected art."

"But you didn't, and you've worked hard and honestly for your living."

"You always support me, darling, please know that I'm grateful." She took a breath and changed gears. "You won't believe what happened at the rotary—I'm thinking of writing a letter to the hotel with a copy to the carabinieri."

"Good lord, what happened?"

"That insipid clerk at the front desk must have tipped off one of those hoodlums on a Vespa who tried to rob me."

"No!"

"Yes, but at the last minute, the French tourists came along and saved me." Natalie then recounted all that had happened at the rotary. Antonella listened intently, but soon her gold-brown eyes filled with amusement, and finally her lips broke into a big smile.

"What's so funny?" Natalie said.

"It's not funny, it's just that he wasn't trying to rob you, he was offering his services.

"What?"

"Yes, sex."

"No! How insulting!" She shook her head, fuming, and then hissed through her teeth, "If I had known that, I would have clubbed him right where it mattered, ruining his career forever!"

"I'm sure you would have."

"That beach isn't safe for women. I'm definitely writing a complaint."

"I was perfectly safe."

"But you weren't! And it only proves you need a husband—a strong man to walk beside you not only on unsafe Italian beaches, but also in Rome at night."

Antonella put up her hand. "*Basta*! You're a broken record on that subject."

"I may be, but I worry about you. Especially now that you're running around with two boyfriends at the same time—that's sex not love."

"Well, I like sex, and it's rare I find a lover. I can't help it that Gene and Lawrence arrived on the same day."

"But now you need to choose one of them, the one with more potential for true love, a long-term relationship."

"Not now. It's only been a few weeks, don't spoil my fun."

"But you must feel more drawn to one than the other."

"I don't. They're totally different and equally attractive. With Lawrence, I love going to clubs and dancing. He moves me around like I'm weightless. And he sings—music lives in him and has to pour out."

"Beware, music and dancing are seductive, they're not

reality."

"His body's reality—he plays soccer in a local league."

"Okay, that's hard to resist…"

"And he's happy, fun loving, affectionate … he actually listens to me."

"A point in his favor. Men rarely listen to women. But why is he called Lawrence?"

"Because he went to the American school where everyone called him Lawrence and Larry—it stuck. His mother's Italian and his father's American, or Polish American."

"Ah, half-Polish like me."

"His dad took his mother's last name when they married, because her family worried 'Rowinski' would deter customers from the family business."

Natalie chuckled. "I can relate to that. I was happy to gain Woody's last name. 'Jablonska' wasn't going to help me make friends or get work here. Anyway, I rather prefer Lawrence to Gene—he's a doctor, stable, undoubtedly wants a family, whereas Gene's a penniless writer and moonlighter."

"He's a trained camera operator. And money doesn't matter when you're falling in love. He turns me on in his big, gruff way. We escape Rome, eat long lunches in the countryside, and then find a deserted meadow where he loosens up. He's like a big lion who goes all soft and sensual after one of those full-course meals. I love being held by him. And I love his dogged ambition, his drive to fulfill his dreams, even when he's down about Italy's privileged barriers to outside talent. My heart goes out to him."

"You can't take on that kind of man—ups and downs,

moods—despite your maternal instinct, which you should put to its proper purpose—children with Lawrence. I know for sure that love sours with a man like Gene. Those jaded types become tyrants, violent in many cases."

"Stop lecturing—I'm dating both for now, and just for now."

"Good. As long as you're aware affairs are based on sexual attraction—egos. The 'in love' state and not true love."

"Yes, I know that, and the in-love state is all I want right now. I've told you before, I don't want to be a married couple. I lived with Dario for five years, and I know for sure I'm happier free. I want my own life and not a second-place existence with constant put-downs and gaslighting from a male partner."

"Bah! You're like a cat in the sun, licking your silky fur. But trust me, I've lived longer and I know about relationships. You won't be young and beautiful forever, at least on the outside, and at sixty, everything changes. By then, you'll have missed out on having children, which is part of a woman's biological blueprint and certainly her greatest fulfillment. Men may let her down, but children live forever in her heart."

"I know you think that, and you know I disagree."

There was a short pause before Natalie made one last attempt. "Don't think I don't know the allure of a new lover—at any age. I still feel those butterflies—there's nothing comparable to falling in love. But at least think of the men. You're not being fair to them, you're not considering their feelings."

"They're feeling what I'm feeling—we're just dating, we're not committed."

"But no man on earth is going to put up with another man

having sex with his woman—even in a casual relationship. Men are territorial. And so are women—would you share your man?"

Antonella sighed. "Okay, you're right, but I'm sure you've juggled more than one crush at a time."

"I have, but I didn't two-time, or not for weeks on end."

"It hasn't been weeks. We have jobs. I've seen them just a few times." Her eyes then lit with a sudden thought. "Hmm, maybe I should suggest a three-way date to avoid two-timing."

"Bad idea."

"Why? Now that I think about it, it's always two gorgeous women in bed with a man. Why not one woman—me—in bed with two gorgeous men?"

"Forget it," Natalie said, but she could see she was speaking to deaf ears. Already, Antonella's gold-brown eyes had soared off to the imagined threesome.

Ménage à Trois

It was Saturday night, nine o'clock, and Antonella was ready for Gene and Lawrence. Her small apartment was a charming turret in an old building near the Colosseum. She had created an evocative atmosphere for the living room with votive candles that pulsed like accompaniments to the soft music humming from the stereo. She had no idea how this experiment would work, but Natalie had been right: her lovers had demanded she choose between them, and she had suggested, with a playful laugh, trying out a threesome. Gene had snorted, and Lawrence had gaped, but the idea had been planted, and now, a week later, they were coming together with curiosity for the novelty of abandoning themselves to the pleasures of sensuality—like the ancient Romans they viewed in movies or read about. It would or it wouldn't work, Antonella thought, as she put two bottles of chilled Prosecco on the coffee table next to three tall, polished glasses. Her lovers were different, and she was the only connection between them. Gene's tension was palpable and partly caused by his unfulfilled dream of producing his own films, which he doggedly wrote at night and that no one ever read. And he had Giorgio, a young son he saw infrequently. As far as she knew, Lawrence had never known hardship. He smiled with a sunny nature that undoubtedly aided his practice as a family doctor. His mother—Alma Gaspari—was from an old Tuscan family known in every household for its olive oil. His father, Stan Rowinski, was a Polish American who had been raised to work in the family's furniture restoration business as soon as he finished college. But he had met Alma when she came for a year to learn English at Boston College. Stan became her round-the-clock English teacher, and Alma returned home pregnant. Stan dropped out of college, moved to Rome, married Alma, and with the wealthy Gasparis' help, the couple opened a fine art restoration and framing studio on via dei Banchi Vecchi. The shop's sign matched the name emblazoned on the family's olive oil label: Gaspari.

The outer doorbell rang, and with a little gasp of fear, Antonella buzzed her gentlemen in. They now had four flights of old stone steps to climb in a narrow spiral, where Gene would have to duck his head at the last turn, because the stone step above it that led to an attic dropped down irregularly, and unsuspecting heads, over hundreds of years, had worn away the marble in that exact spot.

Quickly, Antonella glanced around the room to see what they would see, and then looked at herself one last time in the bedroom's full-length mirror. Her midnight-blue, satin nightgown left her arms and décolletage bare, and she could feel her racing heart just below the gown's low neckline. She wasn't sure she knew that woman in the mirror, who was about to embark on something unknown and scary. "I feel vulnerable," she whispered to the scintillating face in the mirror. "Outnumbered," she added and then laughed, imagining the mirror's seductive figure sandwiched between two virile men. She shivered and then heard male voices rounding the last loop in the stairwell. She went to the door, holding her breath and simultaneously realizing Gene would forget about the low-hanging stair. She heard the crack and his explosive "Fuck!"

"If you need a doctor, I'm here," came Lawrence's bland reply from behind him.

"Asshole! And don't get the idea I'm into this 'little experiment' of hers," Gene growled.

"Ditto, but we said yeah, right? So what the fuck, maybe it'll turn out half-interesting," Lawrence said.

"Said like an Italian. I want tonight to end in a decision—my favor."

"Said just like an Americano," Lawrence said, unfazed. "May the best man win."

The doorbell rang. Antonella counted to five and then swung the door open with a happy smile that conveyed all the nervousness and willingness she was feeling inside. The men stared at her, their jaws momentarily frozen, their competitive mood of seconds before completely forgotten. It was the blue nightgown and her coppery hair, both shining, both dazzling, that paralyzed them. Lawrence woke up first and held out his bouquet of jasmine, prompting Gene to offer his box of chocolates. They stepped through the doorframe at once, but their leather jackets crushed in the middle, preventing entry. Lawrence, not missing a beat, executed a soccer move that cut off Gene and got him to Antonella first. He kissed her cheeks and pressed the jasmine to her chest, the tiny blossoms fanning under her nose. She breathed in the intoxicating scent. Gene bumped Lawrence aside with his height and brawn and wrapped his arms around Antonella in a big American bear hug. "*Bella*," he said, releasing her and giving her the chocolates.

"Oh, thank you, both of you, you two didn't have to bring presents. Come in, I have Prosecco ready, and have a look at Rome's lights, they're so beautiful, like jewels." She led them to the small living area, her nightgown shimmering over her curves as she moved in front of them. Her bare arms and feet, the deep scoop of her gown, her nudity underneath, were enticements for the risky experiment that awaited them.

For a moment, the men just gazed at her traipsing figure while a primal urge rose in them to possess that body, but more than that—to possess it for themselves, own it, as personal property. In that split second, each felt the instinct to shove the other aside with a threatening growl, "Fuck off, loser, she's mine."

As Antonella filled their glasses and felt their possessive vibes, she wondered how they would ever become soft and fuzzy with each other. How would their masculine egos melt away, or enough, to lose themselves in the realm of three-way sensuality? It would be easier with two women and one man—

that combination was easy, part of the time-immemorial patriarchy. She handed them their glasses and said, "To us!" The crystal clinked three ways like wind chimes. They downed their first glass of the bubbly intoxicant but slowed down with the servings that followed. Lawrence turned up the music, and they moved sinuously to it, not exactly dancing, just loosening up while chatting inanely. Soon, as the Prosecco disappeared, they were laughing, joking, and feeling silly. They jostled each other. They warmed up.

Then, finally, with an exultant laugh, Gene swooped Antonella up, spun her around, and headed for the bedroom. Antonella let out a scream of surprise as she was swept off her feet, but then laughed and dropped her head on Gene's chest, feeling her senses swirl. She felt Lawrence's hand close over her ankle as the three of them bumped deliriously into the bedroom and fell wildly on the bed. First kisses and sensual caresses began and quickly led to the men throwing off their clothes and wriggling Antonella's nightgown over her head. She let herself bask in whatever happened next, glad to let the two of them orchestrate everything. Thank God, just this once, for the male-dominated world, she thought. And despite men's generally blind dominance and sexism, she loved them. She loved the way they were made, the shape of their heads as they drove their cars or sat in the theater in front of her, or waited in line at the post office. She loved their hard thighs and buttocks, their broad shoulders and muscled torsos. She loved the hair on their bodies and faces. She loved them unconditionally from her tingling scalp to her excited toes. And now she had two of them holding and caressing her at once. Every touch tantalized her more. Her only awareness was of their combined flesh, their limbs and bodies thrilling to the brain's sensory pleasure. For long, rapturous moments, they moved and rubbed and kissed, hands delighting in everything they felt and explored. With a sensual moan from her deepest recesses, she slid down and breathed in the moist fragrance around Lawrence's navel and just below. In response, high above her, he groaned and gladly surrendered to the exquisite sensation of her lips as they touched his hard phallus. His hands wrapped around her head and held on tight for his building climax. At the same moment, Gene entered her from behind, his hands squeezing her sides, then her breasts, adding to the soaring pleasure of his slow, rhythmic plunges. Enclosed between two beautiful men, Antonella was lost to a sublime dreamland. Lawrence's sighing and groaning and Gene's strong hand traveling up and down her side with deeper and longer thrusts inside her finally drove her to an explosion of blinding fireworks inside her head that rippled, throbbed, and cascaded throughout her body, the walls of her erotic nerve center imploding around Gene's hardness in an ecstatic joy. The sound of her grateful cry set him off with a similar pulsing madness, his mouth thrusting onto Lawrence's. At that fiery fusion, Lawrence also let go with deep, abandoned shudders, his face falling into Antonella. Seconds ticked away. Their bodies subsided slowly and none of them moved. It felt too good, too connected, too remote from reality to interrupt. Antonella lay in the cocoon of her men, utterly content. Slowly, when thoughts began to trickle back to her, she marveled that a man had less chance of satisfying two women at the same time the way a woman could satisfy two men. A smile spread over her face—the power of women.

The phone next to the bed rang, but they ignored it.

Eventually, they came apart but their damp limbs continued to overlap. They murmured a bit, but without intention or relevance. They let the peace continue for as long as it would last. It was the phone that finally forced them up. It rang again.

"Someone really wants to reach you," Lawrence said, "I hope it's not an emergency."

"Said like a doctor," Antonella said.

"It's probably his mother," Gene said.

Lawrence laughed. "Nope, I'm not a *mammista*. I live alone. And she doesn't have Antonella's number—or, not yet." He kissed Antonella's cheek with a big, possessive smile.

Antonella stroked his cheek and sat up to answer the phone. Lawrence rolled to sit next to her, their legs sewn together.

Gene heaved his large frame off the bed and headed for the shower.

Antonella put the phone on speaker, and Natalie's deep, musical voice sailed out. "Toni, I'm so sorry to disturb you, and on Saturday night. Are you alone?"

"What do you think?"

"Is it Gene's night?"

"No, they're both here."

"Damn! What're you up to? Never mind, don't tell me. Or, tell me later. Darling, I'm in a terrible jam, and I can't reach Woody. I didn't want to disturb you, but I can't think of anyone else to call."

"What happened? Are you all right?"

"Yes, except for my nerves. Or, I may be a hostage. Do you remember that man at the ministry café?—the fat one in a black suit who wanted a portrait of his family?"

"Yes, vaguely."

"Well, he sent a driver to bring me here yesterday for the portrait—I'm in his home, but it looks more like a headquarters for a big boss. He's got a couple of boys guarding me, and I noticed one has a gun under his jacket."

"A gun? Where are you? Who is he?"

"Gianni Garella—he handles aircraft for the government. But he must handle other things as well. As soon as I got here, he ran out on urgent business and hasn't come back."

Lawrence leaned forward. "Has anyone threatened you?" he asked.

"Who's that?" Natalie said.

"Lawrence."

"Oh. Well, hello Lawrence, at last we meet—and I hope soon in person. I'm sorry to interrupt your evening."

"No worries, Natalie."

"I saw your sister on the news tonight. She was blasting the government for failing to come through on assistance to rape victims, especially the ones who get pregnant."

"Yup, that's my sister."

"I love her!" Antonella said. "I can't wait to meet her!"

Lawrence put his arm around her. "And she wants to meet you. My whole family does."

"Sounds like a good idea," Natalie said.

Antonella smiled at her friend's constant nudges. "Where are you? Should we be calling the police?"

"No, not yet. No one's actually threatened me. However, these boys wouldn't let me use the office phone till now. They made me stay in the living room, because that's where Garella told them to have me wait until he returned. When I tried to leave as a free citizen, they locked me in. And now, when I finally have a chance to use the phone, I can't get hold of Woody!"

"Give me his number—and his address," Antonella said.

Natalie rattled off Woody's information, while Antonella scribbled it down on the pad by the phone.

"And give us your number and address," Lawrence said.

"I don't know the address. I'm near Ostia, but not right in town. It's rural. I'll ask the boys in the hallway. Wait—there's a flyer on the desk. It's for the Black Rose Club, and Garella's name is on the back. Maybe he owns it. Here's the address—"

The phone went dead.

Antonella sighed. "Maybe she'll call back."

"Sounds pretty weird. But no one's threatening her. Hopefully we can reach her friend."

"I'll keep trying him. Natalie's always in some kind of jam."

Gene came out of the bathroom, a white towel around his waist.

"I hope you left us some hot water," Lawrence said, getting up for his turn in the shower.

"I hope I didn't," Gene quipped back.

Antonella stared at Gene's gleaming body and his fresh

face. "Wow, you should comb your hair more often. You have a lion's head."

He grinned and dropped into the armchair facing the bed, opening his arms for her. "Come here, baby."

"Please don't call me that." But she was only too happy to go to him, the bed's white sheet draped around her like a goddess's robe. She curled up in his lap, and he stroked her like an adored pet. In that warm, cozy moment, she felt safe in his arms.

"Who was it?"

"Guess."

"That dame, your friend that I don't want to meet again."

"Don't say that, I love her."

He nuzzled her hair with affection and murmured gruffly, "I'm crazy about you."

"You're so sexy," she murmured back.

"Mmm, thank you. And I like it best when it's just the two of us."

"But we had so much fun."

"That depends on who you ask. I prefer just the two of us, okay?"

He waited, but Antonella only smiled and kept her head buried in his chest.

"So, what's up with the old lady?"

"Please don't call her that. She's stuck somewhere in Ostia and needs help getting home. She thinks she's with the Mafia and can't reach her ex. We got cut off, but I have Woody's number."

"She must be nuts, how did she end up there?"

"Have you ever heard of Gianni Garella? Involved in aircraft leasing? He hired Natalie to paint his family but then took off and left her with his lackeys."

"Never heard of him, but then again, I'm not rich enough to schmooze with the mobsters. Let's eat, I'm starved." He growled like a bear and dug his teeth facetiously into her shoulder.

"Yes—go eat. I stocked the fridge for you guys. I'm going to shower after Larry."

They got up. Lawrence's singing in the shower could be heard through the open door—a happy, peppy song that covered his full range, the highest notes so sweet. Antonella went into the bathroom and let her drape fall to the floor. Lawrence was just stepping out of the rickety stall—a cheap metal thing added to the centuries-old apartment in the 1980s. His velvety features and dark-lashed eyes were even darker, handsomer, when soaking wet. He laughed seeing her naked and tried to lasso her with his towel, but she dodged him and slid into the shower with a victorious laugh. "There's food," she said as she closed the door, still steamy from the showers before her. But she knew the water from the small tank on the wall would now be quite cool. Lawrence opened the door, stuck his head in, and sang with lovesick eyes lines from the song he had just been singing. She grinned and pinched his nose.

"Ouch," he said and shut the door.

Alone for a few minutes, Antonella slowly turned in the cool spray, especially enjoying the light pellets refreshing her face. She smiled, thinking of Lawrence. She liked him. He was fun and affectionate, always singing, always in motion, but also a good listener, as if he really cared. She knew from his conversation that he came from a close-knit family, where everyone accepted each other, despite their differences—such as his younger sister's career as a globe-trotting student of human sexuality and a leader for women's rights. Italy's deeply entrenched traditions weren't ready for her blunt truths, but the media loved interviewing her, and the public loved her charisma and drama, if not always her views. They also loved her personal story, which she openly described—her brief marriage and divorce to a Neapolitan poet who had threatened her with a butcher knife during a rage attack. She wrote an important paper on domestic violence against women that women applauded and men ignored.

Antonella hadn't grown up in a close-knit family. Rosini was a mad scientist and a mystic, completely absorbed in his research and inventions. He spent hours in his huge lab adjacent to their villa, working alongside several technicians he had trained in the secrets derived from his lifelong study of ancient texts in their original languages—Greek, Egyptian, Sumerian, and Latin. In the lab, he alchemized herbs and roots through vats, tubes, and blazing ovens to produce healing liquids and tablets that filled medicinal bottles embossed with his earthy, holistic Rosini label. But the alchemy also depended on his personal endowment as a divine medium. Through him, the universe transmitted its healing energy into his potions. These carefully composed remedies treated ailing organs, chronic fatigue, and serious disease. Antonella's mother, Jenny, had also devoted her life to mind-body healing and health, training first in yoga, Reiki, and meditation in California, and then traveling to India in search of other therapies and practices. There she had met Rosini at an Ayurvedic conference and become his devotee and partner. Their work was their passion, and they settled in rural Umbria for its pure air and heavenly bodies that nourished the plants. They laid their harvests out on the open hillside to receive the full moon's or the planets' and stars' cosmic energies, depending on the alchemical result being sought. Only rainwater collected in stainless-steel vats could mix with the machine-generated processes in the lab that transformed the plants into elixirs.

At age twelve, Antonella headed off to boarding school in Rome. It had been a horrible moment, leaving home and the tutors who had educated her since early childhood. Along with the cook and housekeeper, the tutors had been her companions. Rosini didn't even say goodbye. He was too busy supervising a driver loading a van with cases of his products. Her mother drove her to Rome, trying to rally her out of her fear and silence with explanations and encouragement that barely touched her, for they were platitudes, lacking sincerity. "I only wish we had schools near home, but we don't," she said. "Be brave, sweetie, life's an adventure, a journey—yours alone. Embrace it! You're setting out today on your very own journey. It's exciting! You're going to have friends, teachers, an international world for your curiosity to explore!"

Antonella had hardly been home after age twelve. Following high school graduation, she moved to Bologna to study foreign languages, interpreting, and translating. From there, she worked long-term at the United Nations in New York, followed by a shorter stint in Brussels, and finally the ministry job in Rome. Over the years, she had dated a number of men and lived with her college boyfriend in both Bologna and New York, but none of the relationships had lasted. And deep down, she hadn't wanted them to. She hadn't wanted to lock herself in. She wanted freedom, options. She wanted men to fall in love with her and for her to fall in love with them. She loved the magical state of falling in love, when no friction, sexism, or boredom infiltrated the relationship—when no extreme effort to feign respect—respect for women, equal status for women—was necessary to maintain the relationship.

She turned off the water and stood there dripping for a moment, wondering if perhaps she had been born to be independent, alone. Gene seemed that way, too, and maybe she had been attracted to him partly for that reason—because he would never make a commitment to her. He had grown up in a dysfunctional family on a ranch in Wyoming, with alcoholic and violent parents. He had escaped to make his own life in film. He had been full of talent and ambition, but alone in the world. She wanted to give to him, douse his alone heart with affection. Lawrence, on the other hand, didn't need that—he gave and received affection naturally. And she loved that side of him. She loved both of them but shuddered at the thought of permanency with either.

Returning her thoughts to Natalie, she got out of the shower. If Woody still didn't answer his phone, then she would drive to his apartment and leave a note on the outside door. She rummaged in her closet for clothes while calling

Woody, but he didn't pick up. She could hear the men talking in the kitchen while she dressed and checked her appearance in the mirror. She saw a woman in love, the glow of it on her face. Her figure was a single line of tights, miniskirt, and cashmere sweater in complementary fall colors. She pulled on brown boots, completing the outfit, and headed to the kitchen, her heels tapping on the hardwood floor.

The men were standing in the tiny kitchen in their underwear, making paninis. They looked at her in surprise.

"Off on your next date?" Gene said.

"Yes, Woody."

"Woody?" Lawrence said.

"He still doesn't answer. I'm going to leave a note on his door. Want to come along?"

Gene groaned. "Let that crone take care of herself."

"You're crass, Gene."

"But I'm not," Lawrence said, waving his butter knife. "I'll take you. I love Rome at night, especially with you on the back of my motorcycle. And besides, you're too pretty to be out on the streets alone at this hour."

"I'm not leaving you alone with her," Gene said. "We'll take my car."

"Fine. Then we'll come back. We're staying over, right, *amore*?" Lawrence said with an expectant face.

"Well ... I wasn't really planning on that."

"No worries, we can take one minute at a time," he said, flashing his friendly smile. He handed her a panino. "I made this one for you."

"Thanks, luv, shall we sit down for a minute?"

Ten minutes later, they were outside, walking the narrow streets of Rome where history breathed from every cobblestone and faded door. The inner streets where Antonella lived were no wider than carriage roads and hardly lit, so that Rome's night enveloped them in its cosmic mystery and seduction. Near the main road, the threesome got into Gene's old station wagon that had a long front seat, allowing them to sit together, Antonella once again in the middle.

It had rained all day, and under the streetlamps of the via dei Fori Imperiali, the road glistened, almost reflected. People were out, shadows flitted across the street, and at Piazza Venezia, larger throngs moved in slow waves toward popular destinations—the Trevi, the Spanish Steps, the Pantheon, and Navona. Across the river, in Trastevere, Saturday night's reveling could almost be heard—its indoor and outdoor parties lasting long past midnight and leaving rubbish strewn in the winding alleys and grimy piazzas.

Gene took side streets toward Piazza Barberini, offering views of quaint nightlife—waiters outside restaurants, serenading passersby about the pasta and fish dishes displayed in their windows and awaiting their palates inside. Rome's energy and enticements never shut down. Under its roads and romantic decay, its furnaces ground all night with an indestructible rumble.

From Piazza Barberini and its Triton fountain, Gene drove up the curving elegance of via Veneto, both sides lined with patchy-skinned plane trees whose branches formed a lacework over the street. Woody lived on a narrow side street near the Porta Pinciana—his old embassy neighborhood—

and Gene pulled right up on the sidewalk by the front door. Lawrence and Antonella got out, and she went to the building's brass plate and rang Woody's bell a few times. When no one answered, she taped her note to the door and went back to the car. Lawrence got in after her and draped his arm over her shoulder. "Mission accomplished, *amore*," he said.

"Yes, but I have an idea. Why don't we drive to Ostia—just for the hell of it—a little adventure—and see if anyone knows where Garella lives, or that club she mentioned, the Black Rose."

Silence answered her. She guessed they were focused on returning to her apartment. "Ha!" she laughed—no chance of that! When the night ended, she wanted to be alone.

"What's so funny?" Lawrence said.

"I don't know, just everything — us, tonight, Rome — Rome's so weird. I love Rome!"

"Yeah … I love it too," Lawrence said.

"*Weird*'s the right word," Gene said, "and I don't want to waste my Saturday night on a wild goose chase for an old lady who's only looking for a midnight ride home."

"I want to help her," Antonella said.

"I'm in," Lawrence said. "It'll be a little adventure, and with you in my arms, I couldn't ask for more—onward, Jeeves!"

"Fuck you."

Nevertheless, Gene pointed the car toward the sprawling lanes of the lamplit Colombo—the road that led south to Ostia. It would be a long night in the car, whizzing past the strange, outlying neighborhoods of the city that bore no resemblance to its ancient core.

Lawrence settled down to nuzzling Antonella with loving murmurs that annoyed Gene. "We'll take turns driving, dude," he said.

"That's okay, I'm used to motorcycles."

"Then you can get some practice with my car."

"It's too big, like a boat."

"It holds my cameras."

Antonella cut it, nudging Lawrence away and changing the subject. "Any news on your application, Gene?"

Gene hissed through his teeth. "Fuck that. They want you to give up your ability with their stupid laws and complicity with the Mafia. They don't want free enterprise. I don't know why I'm still here."

"Giorgio," Antonella said.

"Yeah, I'm here for him."

"So what happened? Did you get turned down for something?" Lawrence said.

"Just about. They haven't formally rejected it, but I'm getting the usual, never-ending runaround that consumes years of my life. No one knows anything except where the waiting room is. Forget doing business here, unless you know someone in the triumvirate."

"It's pitiful. So what's your idea?" Lawrence asked.

"Bah!" Gene said, giving the steering wheel a shake. "I don't even want it anymore. Too much trouble, bad for my health."

"It's for a camera and lighting company, a warehouse to supply production equipment," Antonella said.

"Yeah, I doubt you can break in. It's all controlled."

"But, Christ, competition's healthy—new energy, American innovation. Let a few indies in." He laughed sarcastically.

"Wish I knew someone, dude, but film's not my field," Lawrence said, then added, "but I could ask my sister—she's out there, dealing with celebs—they're her clients."

"It's the laws that have to change. Italy's stuck in its dark ages."

"Sadly."

"At least there's some progress," Antonella said. "That new bill that just passed makes rape a crime against a woman instead of a crime against public morality."

The men made sounds of agreement, and a moment of thoughtful silence ensued. Then Lawrence put his hand on Antonella's cheek and turned her face to him, so she could see his soulful eyes. "I love you. I want to marry you. Would you please marry me, like tomorrow? I want to be with you forever."

Antonella met his gaze with perplexity. She couldn't imagine being married to him—or anyone.

Gene said, "Haven't you noticed, dude, she's not the marrying type."

Lawrence leaned back. "I wasn't talking to you."

"Do you really picture Antonella cooking dinners for you and the kids?" Gene continued, needling him.

"That's not what's important."

"What do you mean? Isn't mealtime the most important thing in your life?"

"No, asshole, it isn't. I cook for myself, and I like cooking. I don't depend on a woman to cook for me and would never ask that."

"You would if you were married, it's in your DNA. Come on, be honest, how often do you stop by mamma's after work for a meal, or how often does she just drop off a casserole kept warm under a dish towel?"

Antonella laughed.

Lawrence ignored Gene and turned back to Antonella. "I want to have children with you, a family. I want to grow old with you. You're what I love and want to care for. I never felt this way before you. And I believe in equality."

She smiled. He was genuine in that natural way of his, and it touched her, especially that he wanted to marry her for love and family life, not just sex. She kissed him. "Thanks, Lar, I can't think about that right now."

"Yeah, give it up, dude, she just gave you a nice 'no,'" Gene said.

Lawrence leaned back again. "I can wait."

His words reverberated in Antonella's head. He could wait. And she could imagine him waiting. In his mind, he had already made her his future wife. He had put the ring on her finger and said with all sincerity in his brown eyes, "I do." She could feel him dreaming their conjugal life—kids, fun times, trips, never-ending quests. She wondered how he would go about changing her mind, fulfilling his goals. Could he really pull it off? Get her to marry him? And wasn't it interesting that Gene wasn't competing for her hand? Marriage wasn't in his head—like her, he was wary of commitment, afraid of the pain, hurt, and trauma involved in relationships, the ones he had experienced since birth and the ones stored in his genetic lineage.

As if the conversation aggravated him, Gene swerved off the road into an abandoned gas station. "Nature calls," he said gruffly, getting out of the car.

"Guess I'll go too," Lawrence said, getting out and following Gene to the wasteland next to the building.

Antonella watched their backs as they peed side by side, Gene of greater height and breadth and Lawrence with his taut, athletic lines. Their heads bobbed back and forth as they talked. Then they zipped up and came back, climbing into the car with a rush of air blowing in with them.

"We were talking," Lawrence said.

"Yeah, and we agree that tonight was interesting, sort of, but we prefer being alone with you. So, you have to choose."

"When?"

"Tonight, or this week at the latest—it's him or me," Gene said.

"Okay," Antonella said.

She saw the men's faces pale at her ready agreement. It meant one of them, or both, would be out of her life forever. She still wanted both. Maybe they could drift along a little longer with their current arrangement. It would buy her time. Choosing one would mean getting serious with the other, and she wasn't ready for that.

They drove on in silence until Gene turned on the radio. A popular song played and Lawrence hummed along, then began singing. Antonella and Gene joined in, and their collective mood rose as they sang louder. When the song ended, they laughed, a togetherness infusing their spirits.

As they neared Ostia, the flat barren land stretched into the depths of night with an eerie, low-lying fog. "Pretty weird out here," Antonella said. "A little scary."

"Maybe this creep who's got your friend lives out there, and you're picking up his vibes," Gene said.

Lawrence took her hand and held it on his thigh, as if to say, "you're safe with me."

At the first sign of civilization—a roadside bar with youth hanging out in a courtyard with empty tables and chairs—Antonella told Gene to stop. "Let's see if anyone knows Garella or the Black Rose Club."

Gene pulled over, getting the attention of the young people.

"They're too young," Lawrence said, but rolled down his window anyway. "Hey, *amici*, excuse me—we're looking for a friend of ours—Garella, Gianni. Do you know where he lives?"

The teenagers tossed around the name, but ultimately shrugged apologetically. Then one of them called out, "*Un attimo*," and went inside where other young people were playing arcade games. The bar's owner, a graying man wearing a short black apron, stepped outside and squinted hard at Gene's car and its passengers while drying his hands on a white dish towel. Then he flapped the towel in the southerly direction.

"Garella? You want Garella, Gianni? Try the Black Rose Club, that way—left, then right, then left, but before the beach." He didn't actually say the words "left" and "right," but flapped his towel in those directions—this way, that way, this way. It was the Italian way to give directions—by waving the arms—or by walking ahead of a car through the first few turns.

"Why can't he just give us street names with landmarks, the logical American way," Gene said.

"I got it," Lawrence assured him, as he gave the bar owner a thumbs up.

Gene drove on and Antonella smiled at him. "I can't believe we found him first try."

"But we're not looking for him, we're looking for her," Gene said. "And we're going to need a story."

"I'll say she's my mother," Antonella said.

"Nope, she's gotta be Lawrence's mother. Italians feel sorry for men looking for their mothers."

Lawrence laughed. "True, but come on, every culture on the planet feels sorry for its men. We could say *you're* looking for *your* mother."

"No, Gene doesn't look like he had a mother," Antonella said.

"I would've been better off," Gene said.

"You actually look like a bouncer," Lawrence said. "And the bouncers at this club aren't going to like competition. They won't help us if it's you looking for your mother. I agree, we'll be looking for mine, and Antonella's my little sister. That'll really get them—me, taking care of all the women in my family."

They laughed.

A few minutes later, still on the outskirts of town, they arrived at the blazoning pink and blue neon sign of the Black Rose Club, the rose itself black and outlined in diamond lights. The parking lot was full of cars, motorcycles, and scooters. Gene squeezed into a spot, and the trio headed for the front entrance. Men and women hung out in groups in the courtyard, talking and smoking cigarettes. They dressed elaborately, theatrically, and some of the women wore highly styled hairdos that, as they got closer, turned out to be wigs. All eyes stared at the newcomers as they came up the flagstone walk to the door. Strangers.

Two men in dark clothing greeted them with implacable faces, checked their IDs, and grudgingly admitted them. Inside, past the foyer, the place was huge, low-ceilinged, and dimly lit, with disco music blaring. Café tables surrounded a dance floor, where dizzying laser lights in neon colors swept across the floor, the walls, and the ceiling like sword blades. Revelers danced intensely, their faces stabbed by the attacking lights. Waiters in black and white worked the tables, supplying drinks and snacks. It was a noisy, pleasure-seeking scene.

"I hate this kind of music," Gene shouted.

The others nodded, feeling tortured by the electronic buzz vibrating through their bodies.

"Come on, let's ask at the bar," Gene said and led the way to the far side of the room, where weakly glowing lamps hung in a long line above the bar. As they wove through the crowd of heavily made-up men and women, Antonella was reminded of Venice during Carnevale. Only masks were missing.

Gene bent down with cupped hands to make a megaphone. "Everyone's in drag."

Antonella and Lawrence nodded.

At the bar, Gene leaned over the counter and asked the

bartender where he could find Gianni Garella. The bartender stared at him suspiciously and may have stepped on a hidden buzzer, for within seconds, two security guards arrived and the one who was the boss said, "What do you want?"

"Why hello," Lawrence said genially, while pulling out his medical ID. "I'm Dr. Gaspari, and my mother, Signora Edwards, came to Signor Garella's house yesterday to paint a portrait of his family. But now, my stepfather—my mother's husband—has suffered a heart attack and is in intensive care in Rome. I need to take my mother there. He might not make it. And I don't have a phone number for Signor Garella."

The guards exchanged a look, and then the boss said, "Signor Garella isn't here. And you're the signora's son?"

"Yes, and this is my little sister, her daughter."

"And him?"

"Oh … he's Eugenio, my mother's driver, my mother's manservant. He drove us here."

Antonella suppressed a laugh, and Gene's face flashed indignation.

The head guard took his time deciding what to do and finally huffed irritably. "Bah … come with me."

As soon as they got to the foyer, which was quieter, Gene fell into step with him. "Hey, signore, I was wondering, have any films been shot here?"

The guard shook his head.

"What a location. I can picture some great scenes."

He dropped back to Antonella and Lawrence. "I've got an idea for a new script," he said. "The owner of a trans club is a secret drag queen. He can't come out because his Mafia connections would kill him for sexual deviance, especially being a married man. His lover's a popular entertainer—a beautiful Korean trans woman—and she helps him build a sexy club out here in the middle of nowhere. That way he has a safe place to be his true self. The scenes jump back and forth between his two worlds—the real one at his club and the fake one with the Mafia. But things get dangerous because there's a rat, a repressed gay man. He starts spying. By this time, the audience really likes our hero—he's good to marginalized people, cares about his community, generously shares his wealth. When the Mafia assassinates him, he's died for his cause, and ultimately we come out of the theater with better understanding of different sexualities."

"I like it—my sister would definitely publicize it for you."

"I gotta meet your sister."

"No way you're going near her. Only through me."

"Look!" Antonella cried. There, across the courtyard, was an orange telephone booth, and inside was Natalie, her ash-blonde hair as bright as the overhead light bulb.

"Natalie!" Antonella called out, running to the booth.

The petite woman started in surprise, then stared in wonder at Antonella before fumbling her way out of the booth. She wore a pale blue suit with a pale gray raincoat over it and dainty black pumps on her feet. "Toni! Good God, how on earth did you find me?"

The reunion was happy and affectionate. Lawrence hugged Natalie as if she were his dear, beloved mother, and Gene gave a more subservient bow, both gestures for the sake of the guards, who were looking on with appreciative smiles, pleased to have played a role in this family reunion. But, not wanting to appear too friendly, they turned back to their club duties with a wave over their shoulders. Antonella called after them, "Thank you, signori, thank you so much for helping us!" The others echoed her words and the guards waved again, with warmer smiles.

"It's truly a miracle you found me," Natalie said, putting her hands on the men's arms. "I'm so delighted to see you," she said. "I glimpsed you at the wedding, but now I fully understand why Antonella can't choose between you. I would have trouble myself."

Antonella put her arm around Natalie. "What a night, Nat! Come on, we're taking you home."

They set off for the parking lot, Natalie all excited. "I can't believe it's over. I can't believe I looked up and there you were. I felt sure something terrible was brewing after my host disappeared yesterday."

"He probably got a call from Palermo," Gene said.

Natalie laughed. "Whatever it was, he forgot to tell those stupid boys of his that I wasn't being held for ransom. They locked me in. They said Garella had told them I was to wait until he returned. Finally he came back tonight, probably around the time you were arriving here. But let me calm down for a minute, and then I'll tell you all."

Gene opened the car's back door for Natalie. "Hop in, signora, at your service." He gave a little bow.

"Why thank you, Gene."

"Lawrence told the guards he was your manservant," Antonella said.

Natalie laughed. "A permanent position, I hope!" She looked playfully at Gene. "What I need now, my dear man, is a double scotch."

"Coming right up, milady," he said with another little bow and headed for the driver's door.

"There's a bar up the street," Antonella said, "which is how we found the club."

Natalie pulled her legs into the car. "You wouldn't believe Garella's house—it's like one of those drug lord's haciendas you see in American movies. It connects to the club through those fields." She waved at the dark, foggy fields behind the club. "I ran through them to get here. It was horrible—all thorns and rocks. Don't look at my legs!" She reached down and rubbed her shins through her nylons.

"Are you hurt?" Lawrence asked, leaning into the car. "Shall I have a look?"

"How fortunate to have a doctor on hand," Natalie said, extending her right leg. "But I'm sure I merely shredded my nylons."

Lawrence's trained fingers ran over her shinbone and around the ankle. "I don't feel any bad bruises, and I don't see any scrapes. How about the other leg?"

She twisted to produce the other leg. He pressed a few places, but Natalie shook her head—no pain.

"Good, and looks like your stockings survived the torture. But wait, what's this bandage on your left knee?"

"Oh … just something I stupidly did the other day. I caught my heel in the cobblestones outside Rosati's."

"You mean you fell. And you know you shouldn't be wearing heels in Rome, not even these pumps."

"Yes, I know that, Dr. Gaspari, but I feel too ordinary in flats, and I was meeting an important gentleman for an aperitif."

"But you can learn a new habit. And we men wear flats too. And we like women in flats. Flats are sexy."

She laughed. "Don't give me that, but *va bene*, you've made your point. I promise to try, *dottore*." She smiled demurely.

He patted her shoulder and drew out of the car. Then, remembering something, he bent back down and asked, "What about shock? Do you have any shock?"

"No, none. I actually feel quite fine. I've dealt with far worse—perhaps Antonella's told you my story. But I'll feel a lot better when I get that double scotch."

"Good, we're off," he said, straightening.

Antonella was right there, and he kissed her cheek. "She's fine, scotch next stop."

"I'll ride with her," Antonella said.

Minutes later, they sat around one of the outdoor tables at the same bar where they had been given directions, but this time with their jackets zipped up because of the nippy fall air. It was long after midnight, but the bar was still busy with youth, inside and out, though the new arrivals were the only ones seated at a table. The bartender was glad to see them again and learn that his directions had led to a successful mission. He came back with their drinks—on the house—scotch for Natalie and Gene and amaro for Antonella and Lawrence.

Natalie sipped with desire and relief. "I had five minutes

with Garella yesterday before he left on that emergency call. And he wasn't in regular clothes when he received me. He wore a black robe and looked exactly like an Orthodox priest from historical paintings. He was friendly and we discussed the portrait he wanted, but he acted distracted the whole time. Then one of his men came in and said he had an important call, and that was the last I saw of him until tonight. Yesterday, I was served dinner in the living room where I had been told to wait, always expecting him to return any moment. Then I fell asleep on the couch, and when I woke up in the middle of the night I found the door locked. The windows had bars, and there was no phone in the room. I banged on the door and yelled for help. Finally one of those boys came and opened it. He said I had to wait for Garella, those were his orders."

Natalie drained her scotch. "Today was endless. I refused all food. I read magazines without knowing what I read. I did exercises. I inspected my quarters minutely for a way to escape. I begged through the closed door to use a phone to call my family, but no one answered me. Tonight, when I couldn't take it anymore, I took one of Garella's smaller statues and clubbed the door with it. One of the boys finally opened it and let me use the office phone. That's when I called Woody, and then you, my dear Antonella. How lucky you were home, and all of you came to save me." She patted Antonella's hand on her left side and then held up her empty glass to Gene on her right.

"Shall we have another, darling? I really feel like getting drunk tonight."

"I'll keep you company," Gene said, taking her glass and

getting up. "What about you guys?"

"Sure," Lawrence and Antonella chimed.

Gene went inside and soon returned with the drinks. Natalie sipped hers with a grateful thirst that showed in her face. Then she said, "There's one last piece to this story, if you'll indulge me."

"I definitely want to hear it," Gene said.

"Good, thank you for letting me purge." She took a sip, then a breath, and continued. "So, when Garella finally showed up, I was so relieved I wanted to hug him but also punch him. He apologized profusely. He said things had gotten out of his control, he'd been detained without access to a phone, and his boys had misunderstood, but now, everything was back to normal. 'Signora, I promise to make it up to you,' he told me. 'My private plane is outside, and we'll fly to my villa in Malta—no more than an hour away. I promise you'll love it there—you can paint the portrait without any interruptions. And the property has a small chapel that I'd like you to see. I was hoping you might also paint frescoes for it. They could even be of the family, if you prefer. My wife is already there and has your apartment ready—fully equipped with clothes, toiletries, and anything else you might need or find lacking. The children are there too, everyone's eager to meet you.'"

"*Ma dai*! Did that really happen?" Antonella said.

"It most certainly did."

"I gotta meet this guy—maybe he'll back my new script— the one I'm writing about the Black Rose," Gene said.

"Why did you have to escape if he was being so nice?"

Lawrence said.

"Because I was terrified he'd roll me up in a carpet and put me on the plane to Malta! Luckily he got another one of those calls, and I bolted. Outside, I could see the club's lights in the distance, through the fog, and I ran for them as if they were the Swiss border."

"Do I have permission to write my version of your story, signora?" Gene asked.

"You have my blessing," Natalie said and toasted him with her amber drink.

The others toasted too and finished off their last sips, but no one made a move to get up. Sitting outside in the chilly, tingling mist, far from the city, under a vast night sky on the ancient shores of Rome felt too good to give up. The effects of the alcohol enhanced the pleasure. And Natalie had been cooped up in frightened solitude for hours, so that now, she was in no hurry to end the warmth of freedom, friendship, laughter, and safety. She had Gene on her right, Antonella on her left, and that handsome doctor with gorgeous eyes facing her across the table and smiling whenever their eyes met. More than that, café tables had always been a highlight in her life—people, being with people. That's why she loved painting them. But these three young people—already half-way through their lives—were still single, and that disturbed her. The quadruple scotch had loosened her tongue, and she said, "I can't imagine how you're managing this ménage of yours. I would find it perfectly unbearable," she said. "Nature intended intimacy and partnership between a man and a woman, not a group."

"Are you saying only between a man and a woman?" Antonella said.

"No, I just meant two people, though personally I can't imagine anything but a man and a woman."

"We gave her an ultimatum," Gene said.

"Well, thank God, though I hope we can all remain friends—"

"A voice I know only too well," a man's self-assured voice said, as his shoes crunched on the gravel path to the patio. All heads turned to look at the elegant, older gentleman in a trench coat and hat who approached them.

"Woody!" Natalie cried out in amazement. "How did you find us?"

"Natalie, it's the middle of the night, and I can't believe I'm barely back in Rome, and already I'm getting you out of some crazy scrape."

He arrived at their table where everyone had risen to greet him. Natalie made introductions, and words flew back and forth to describe to Woody all that had happened to Natalie.

"It's going to be a great screenplay," Gene said. "I've already started writing it up here." He tapped his head with his finger.

Woody smiled. "I don't doubt it'll be a blockbuster. And if you throw in her early life, followed by her marriage to me, you'll have an epic of grand proportions."

Everyone laughed.

"I hate to cut this short, but it's late and I'm tired. I somehow lasted through a four-hour Wagner opera. But I look forward to seeing all of you again and thanking you properly for helping Natalie," Woody said with a sincere smile and good set of teeth.

"Yes! Lunch at the club," Natalie said. "How about next Sunday?"

They all agreed, though Antonella wondered if the lunch would still happen if her love life changed.

Natalie slid her arm through Woody's, and her voice purred contentedly. "I'm so glad you'll get to know Woody, who's ever so charming when I haven't annoyed him."

Woody rolled his eyes, and Natalie grinned up at him. Then, arm in arm, they headed off to the parking lot.

A few minutes later, the friends were back on the road to Rome, the misty night all around like a mysterious, animate universe so much bigger and inexplicable than themselves. Lawrence snuggled up to Antonella, and she rested against him. His body melded so naturally to hers and was warm with a beating heart. She could feel his smile against her head. Soon he murmured affectionately, "I like Natalie's philosophy—partnership, family, love."

Gene heard and cut in, "Love equals pain. Torture. Despair."

Lawrence lifted his head. "You need help, my sister can give you a referral."

"Bug off, *porco*."

Lawrence dropped back into the ripples of Antonella's hair. She was dozing now, a contented smile on her lips. He was feeling deep contentment himself, like his battle to win her was almost over. Their adventure that night had brought them closer together, with Gene slightly to the side.

As for Antonella, her mind was drifting in that liminal

state before sleep, where odd images and voices surfaced and disappeared. A male voice spoke from nowhere, invisibly. "The horizon's gray." She came to for an instant and thought, Yes, the night's fading from dark depth to surface gray, same as our ménage. The night's transcendence is ending, it exists only in darkness, only in night's unruled realm. She dozed off again, and an old peasant woman in black materialized. She held out her aged hand, and in the palm Antonella saw two shining gold coins. The woman smiled and said, "They're waiting for you."

Antonella woke up and wondered who was waiting for her. Why the gold coins with those words? Did the old woman mean children?

As if on cue, Lawrence gathered her close and cradled her. "*Amore*," he said, and she felt his love flow into her.

Gene drove on in silence, shoulders relaxed for a change. His mind was buzzing with new ideas. He was already writing the drag queen Mafia script in his head and thinking how he would talk to Woody about it at their lunch on Sunday. Maybe Woody had investor connections back in the States. Maybe Fellini's costume designers were still around. He felt an enormous surge of motivation and ambition to get home to his desk and start writing.

As they approached the city walls, passing the ghostly Caracalla Baths, Antonella roused, not wanting to miss the ancient sights as they reentered the city—the broken arches and temples, the battered columns and fragments of buildings, the gigantic arena—all of Rome's relics standing higher and nobler than any later construction—the baroque palaces, the domed churches and campaniles, and the magnificent sculptures and fountains. Rome of the Romans still dominated the inner city and took the breath away.

Antonella and her companions stared out the windows in silence, feeling the triumphal force that held them spellbound. Rome's engines had purred through the night and were now stoking up for another day of human activity on the planet.

Marriage

Months passed, another year, and soon it was early spring. The days were getting longer, the sun was setting later, and Romans were beginning to eat outside again and wander the streets late at night, the city's mysterious magic once again permeating every dark byway and flow of water from shadowy fountains and curbside hydrants.

Lawrence and Antonella had married in October of the previous year. They lived in the hills above the Farnesina, in a gated condominium complex with grounds like an arboretum. Lawns and paths wove through the handsome brick buildings, with umbrella pines, magnolias, palms, flowering shrubs, and fragrant vines. It was a lush and exclusive environment.

The newlyweds' second-floor apartment was spacious with an open design. Antonella had wanted to remain in her cozy turret near the Colosseum, but Lawrence's parents had pressed them to take the family's extra apartment that for years had been rented to the Swedish Embassy. It was just waiting for one of the Gaspari children to marry and move in. The elder Gasparis lived in the same complex—Lawrence and his siblings had grown up there. His younger brother, Matteo, still lived at home, but was in the States pursuing a double masters' in business and art history. He planned to join his parents in the family's art and framing business. Donatella, the middle sibling, lived in Trastevere, Rome's hipper, more bohemian neighborhood that suited her temperament and taste. So, the large apartment had fallen to the newlyweds. And once Antonella saw the amount of Lawrence's belongings, which included a treadmill and a piano and paintings inherited from his great-grandfather, she realized the bigger place was necessary. "And we'll have children," Lawrence liked to tease her in his smiling, buoyant way, knowing she did not want children and had agreed to marriage only if he agreed to just the two of them. And he had agreed, his brown eyes doleful every time he nodded "yes," but behind those warm and loving eyes, he hoped he'd be able to change her mind, or if too much time passed, allow an accident to happen with their birth control.

It was Friday night, the workweek done, and Lawrence was waiting for Antonella to return from a weeklong summit in Brussels. He was excited to see her, his heart pumping—no, overflowing—with the natural love he felt for her. His mother, Alma, was bringing over a pan of *carciofi alla romana*—Antonella's favorite. It was a homecoming welcome. Antonella's addition to the family had been warm and affectionate on both sides. Everyone loved her and she loved them. Many a night the two couples ate dinner together, sometimes walking down the street to their favorite restaurant near Ponte Milvio. It was only Lawrence who sometimes sensed that Antonella held back the deepest part of herself, the part that might fully connect with him the way his love fully merged with her. It was as if she were transient, there for now but the future unknown.

The doorbell rang and his mother arrived with the artichokes, Donatella, in tow. "Oh, Mamma," Lawrence made a swooning face for the aroma of the artichokes, "smells divine, thank you so much!" He kissed Alma and took the pan from her. She was a petite woman, her trim figure always dressed neatly in a skirt, blouse, and cardigan sweater. Her short silvery hair was neatly coiffed. Long ago it had been the glossy ebony of Lawrence's, and their resemblance was easily detected. Alma had a naturally generous nature — for everyone—and although she ran the family business with Stan, she always had time for family and friends.

Donatella was tall and lanky like her Polish father, but fully Italian with her beauty and glamour. She had to bend a little to exchange kisses with Lawrence, and her energy blew on him as she did so. "Bro, I want to see your place now that you've fixed it up," she said.

"Good. Come to the kitchen first," he said, leading the way.

"Where's Antonella?" Alma said, as they passed through the narrow hallway that connected to the kitchen.

"Late. And she's not picking up, nor is Alitalia."

"That's nothing new," Donatella said, meaning the airline.

Lawrence put the pan onto the counter and lifted one

corner of the dish towel covering it. "I have to have just one," he said, popping a plump, succulent artichoke into his mouth, biting it off at the stem. "Mmm," he sighed happily with eyes closed.

"I'll have one too," Donatella said, lifting the cloth.

"That's all!" Alma said, taking the pan and putting it in the oven out of reach. "I made these for Toni. She's been hard at work all week."

"So have we, Mamma," Donatella said.

"I know that," Alma said with a smile, reaching up to stroke Donatella's cheek, "and I'm so proud of both of you."

"Come on, I'll give you a tour, but it's barely furnished— Toni's a minimalist."

"Me too," Donatella said, "the opposite of you, ha ha. But I was hoping to see Toni, we have a big conference coming up in May and need interpreters."

"I'm sure she'll want to help," Lawrence said, as they came back to the spacious front hallway with gleaming dark wood floors. "I call this the central nave, since everything leads off of it," Lawrence said. At its head lay the living room—two armchairs and a couch, with a coffee table between them. The dining room lay to its right with a door to the kitchen. The apartment's largest balcony ran along these two spaces, behind picture windows and a sliding glass door. Fanning palms and a striped canopy gave privacy to the balcony. Along the left side of the front corridor, a square archway with sliding paneled doors led to a den with another balcony and a second bedroom and bathroom.

"The kids' room," Donatella said.

"Yeah, I wish."

Donatella looked at Lawrence. "No change of heart yet?"

"I'm working on it."

"Give her time. Her childhood affected her trust—that's a big deal."

"I know, but I'm so ready for kids."

"Me too!" Alma laughed.

"Want me to talk to her?" Donatella said.

"No."

"Yes!" Alma said.

"I think she's afraid marriages don't last, and then there'd be kids who suffer."

"And she's right," Donatella said. "Most people get married when they're passionately in love, and a lasting relationship isn't about sexual desire—that part doesn't last."

"Well, maybe I can get her to have kids while there's still sexual desire," Lawrence said.

"Ha—exactly what she might be afraid of."

They smiled at each other, believing this was only a short-term problem soon to be resolved.

Their last stop was the master suite, situated next to the front door. It had its own little hallway that connected the bedroom at one end and a study at the other, with a bathroom between. The bedroom had yet another balcony, and the study housed Lawrence's treadmill.

"Time to get rid of that thing," Donatella said. "Toni needs an office."

"I was thinking the same thing."

"Great space, bro, I'm happy for you. And if you're free

next week, let's get together for dinner, my place. You too, Mamma, you and Papa."

They came back to the front door and with another round of kisses agreed to be in touch about a date for the following week. Then the women left, and Lawrence paused for a moment, thinking of what he could do while waiting for Antonella—steal another artichoke? The pan was full. Just as he turned to step toward the kitchen, the doorbell rang again. He assumed the women had forgotten something, but when he opened the door he found his nemesis, Gene, standing there, no—swaying there like a tall tree about to topple over.

"Fuck, what're you doing here? Are you drunk?"

"Save me, bro." He stumbled in, bumping past Lawrence.

"Hey, you can't come in, I have plans!" he pulled on Gene's sleeve.

"I just need ten. I drove into the wall at your lower gate. We've been shooting DiCaprio's new film all week, and I haven't slept in days. I gotta have ten minutes before I drive again. Come on, be nice. Doctors are supposed to help people."

He staggered into the master suite.

"Hey! Do not go in there! Shit, you stink, like garbage!" Lawrence said, wrinkling his nose in disgust.

"Yeah, I know, sorry." He was already pulling off his clothes and heading for the bathroom.

"Hey! I said no!"

"A quick shower, a little sleep, and I'll be outta here!"

"No, asshole!" Lawrence briefly tussled with naked Gene before throwing up his arms in disgust. "You prick!"

Gene got into the shower and groaned with pleasure as

the water sprayed on his face. To needle Lawrence, he called out in his wicked way, "Where's Toni? Where's that doll? I could use some of her TLC right now, mmm-mmm. And I got a whiff of those artichokes—hell, I'm starved!"

In the little hallway, Lawrence growled and kicked Gene's clothes into a ball. He found a plastic bag and pushed them in. He wanted Gene out of there before Antonella got home, otherwise they might be stuck with him for dinner. He went to the kitchen and got the artichokes out of the oven. Unnerved, angry, he ate one of the soft, juicy bulbs, but couldn't taste it because of his mood. He now hoped Antonella would be late. After their one experimental night together long ago, Antonella had made her choice—him—and though the three of them occasionally saw one another, Lawrence made a serious effort to avoid Gene. He couldn't stand the way Gene touched and kissed Antonella whenever they said hello and goodbye. He hated the way Gene looked her over and flirted with sexy innuendos—quips intended as much to annoy Lawrence as to tease Antonella. Worse, Antonella flirted back, despite her abhorrence for chauvinistic behavior. And that was the crux. Lawrence knew, but hated to admit it, that Gene was the kind of bad-boy guy that women automatically loved, even though they didn't trust the type and were treated badly by the type. It was something physically magnetic about the Gene-type, and the Gene-types knew their power over women.

Lawrence picked up the kitchen phone and called Antonella's cell phone, and then tried Alitalia, but didn't reach either. He went back to the master suite to hustle Gene on his way—surely the shower woke him up enough to drive the remaining kilometers to his home in Rome's *campagna*. The bathroom door was open, with swirling steam inside. Big wet footprints led to the bedroom. Gene was sprawled face down on the matrimonial bed, his skin fresh and damp, with beads of water at the base of his spine and on the golden down of his legs.

"Get up, you fucking bastard, and hit the road," Lawrence said and picked up Gene's towel from the floor.

Gene grumbled into the pillow without moving. Then he turned his mouth just enough to say, "I'm like lead, dude, seriously, give me ten, that's all I'm asking for." Then he added in his devilish way, "Mmm, this pillow smells so good, like Toni."

"Out!" Lawrence whipped Gene's ankles with the wadded towel.

Gene rumbled with a laugh but didn't move.

"You make me sick, you creep," Lawrence said, but he didn't pursue it further—maybe it *was* safer to let him catch a few winks before driving again. He looked at his watch to mark the time and took a last glance at the body on the bed. No doubt it was an amazing human specimen, even at forty-one, with fatigue settling into areas of the flesh. The broad, muscled shoulders tapered down the long spine, and then the flesh rose up to full, sensual buttocks, followed by long, manly legs, everything in proportion. He left the room, blinking to clear his sight, especially the strange memory of being entwined with those same limbs, along with Antonella's, in a sublime state that he could not imagine—it could only be experienced.

Back in the little hallway, he noticed light coming from under the closed study door. But when he looked in, he found the light was coming from the next-door neighbor's balcony. It jutted out, giving the neighbors a full view into the study with its treadmill. They were hosting a dinner party that night, with lamps and flaming heaters lighting the space. Lawrence saw Natalie and Woody among the guests at the table and heard tinkling conversation and pleasant laughter. He closed the door before anyone noticed him.

Lawrence turned back, checked his watch, and went back to the bedroom to plunk down in the armchair by the window and wait for Gene's time to be up. He did not want Antonella finding Gene sprawled naked on their bed. Folding his hands under his chin, his faced the sleeping body. Soon, his thoughts inevitably drifted to the miracle and mystery of human sexuality. Humans varied so much, and perhaps they were born bisexual, but grew up developing a stronger preference one way or the other, or in whatever way. He loved women, unquestionably, but over his lifetime had noticed a few men, not in a pressing way where he felt a need to pursue them. No, not at all, just in his imagination. And he didn't feel ashamed about it—desire was natural, an ever-present drive in the human organism. Only once had he experienced sex with a man—the man lying in front of him on the bed. And everything about those moments, experienced in a blindly exquisite state, he could no longer fathom. But what if the state were reactivated? Desire—following it, satisfying it— took place in a different mental realm. What would happen if he sat down on the edge of the bed—like a good friend, or the healer he was—and massaged those tight, stressed shoulders? Gene would groan with the pain, but also in gratitude for the helping touch. Lawrence's hands would work out those knots, and then knead each vertebra down the spine, and as the seconds passed, the bodily contact between them would arouse a sensual connection that altered reality. Eventually, his hands would reach the fabulous buttocks and press down on them. It would be then that both of them would consider the question of "what if?" What if they surrendered to the delicious sensations? Desire's delights? Lawrence grinned behind his folded hands. He would love to control that powerhouse of a man weakened by the throes of desire—that brash character who in regular life stepped on others without a shred of remorse. Lawrence nodded with a laugh, remembering Hadrian and Antinous, Apollo and Hyacinthus, and Achilles and Patroclus— human nature's sensual, hedonistic, and homoerotic drive that ancient Greeks and Romans lived openly and continued to this day in Rome's secret lairs. But not here. He got up and shook the mattress. "Time's up. Hit the road, Jack, and don't come back."

Meanwhile, Antonella had arrived at the airport, her cell phone dead and her mood impatient to get home. At the taxi stand outside the terminal, two drivers argued with obscene language and hand gestures over who would take her home. While they shouted their insults—a whole history of them going back years—a gray-haired, elfin man took her bag and in his high-pitched, fast-flowing Italian told her to follow him.

"Come with me, signorina. They're *malandrini*, thieves. They'll charge you 150,000 lira to go to your hotel."

"But they're at the taxi stand."

"Yes, but they're fakes. They pay the police." He twirled his hand in the air—"This is Italy. This is Rome. But my taxi's registered, it has a meter. You can trust me."

Moments later, the little man was driving her at reckless speed along the airport's autostrada toward Rome. His head barely rose above the steering wheel, and he kept looking high up to see Antonella through the rearview mirror—in fact, it was pointed at her and not the rear window. His hands bounced on and off the wheel to dramatize the story he was telling, as she sat imprisoned in his car.

"She was Viennese, a lady like you—*bella, simpatica*—and I saved her from thieves just like the ones who were trying to rob you. I told her if she wanted to go to Tivoli the next day, I could take her for 125,000 lira. She said yes, and, oh *Dio*, what a day we had—walking and talking as if time didn't exist. I don't need to tell you what happened when we got back to her hotel that night. It was beyond this world. She was married but invited me to visit her in Vienna. She borrowed a friend's apartment, and for three days we never left each other's arms!" His oily, slitted eyes met Antonella's in the mirror. "I know how to please women, *capisce*?"

Antonella changed the subject. "We had nothing but rain in Brussels. It's so good to be back in Rome."

"Yes, Rome, the most romantic city on earth, full of beautiful women, and I know all the special places to take them." He drew a hungry breath and eyed Antonella with a lascivious grin. She kept her eyes averted, but he could not stop himself. "Another time, it was here in Rome that I fell in love. It was with an American woman, a diplomat, a distinguished lady like you. But our affair couldn't last. Rome looks big, but it's actually small, and we knew one of those spies from her embassy would notice us. But I'll never forget our late-night strolls that always ended at the Trevi for gelato."

Again he tried to meet her eyes in the mirror, but she was staring out the window. Her mind was fixated on the neighborhoods they were passing and how much time remained till she reached hers. She was sure the poor bastard wouldn't touch her. He was feeding off his fantasies and delusions and needing to boast about them. Nevertheless he was harassing her by running his eyes continually over her and making inappropriate sexual conversation. And it wasn't over yet.

"Your husband's a lucky man." He licked his lips, as if tasting her. "I hope he knows it, but usually husbands neglect their wives. But I'm different, I understand women, and they know it. They respond. I can tell you're electric—electric! I can feel it! And when I love a woman, my love is lavish. I'm not cheap."

His tires screeched as he took the turn into the condominium complex's back entrance that led to a security gate. She regretted having given him her address. She should have told him to let her out at the corner instead. Feeling a stab of nastiness toward the man she had been forced to endure for thirty-five minutes, she said, "So, you never married?"

Self-pity immediately hung in his shoulders and head. "No, it never worked out that way. Something always came up, pulling us apart, even though we wanted to stay together."

The guard at the gatehouse recognized Antonella and

waved the taxi through. The driver parked in front of her building and put her bag down by the tall, locked gate. She thanked him coolly and punched in the code to release the lock. As she pushed through the gate, she heard his syrupy voice singsong to her back, "*Ciao, bella, carissima.*"

She continued on without a backward look, remembering how long ago a small, yappy dog had bitten her leg only after she had walked past it. The heavy wood gate swung shut with loud finality.

It was getting late, and Antonella was tired and hungry, glad to be home, glad to be seeing Lawrence again, now her closest friend to whom she could confide. He always listened and responded. He was curious and cared. She drew in a deep breath of the intoxicating *Pittosporum,* whose lush white blossoms bordered the flagstone walk to the condo's entrance. *Pittosporum* was the most powerful scent in the hills where she lived, especially at night, as if the dark sky's infinity drew and diffused its fragrance. She took the elevator to the second floor and was surprised to find Max Wagner, the Austrian ambassador to the Vatican, about to ring her doorbell. He and his wife, Sandra, a former Italian model, and their young son, Dino, lived below them on the first floor.

"Antonella! I was just coming up to ask a favor of Lawrence." His toothy grin flashed at her. He was quite attractive, in his late forties, with wavy gray hair brushed back from his suntanned forehead. He and Sandra often appeared in the society pages of the local newspapers. Before meeting and marrying Sandra, he had worked for many years in Washington and New York, and as a result dressed like an Ivy League

American when he wasn't in the office. He now looked as if he had just returned from an American country club or barbecue, for he wore a pink polo shirt with a green alligator over the heart, yellow khaki pants, and New England Top-Siders.

He gestured to her suitcase. "Were you in Brussels?"

"Yes, the summit, I'm bushed."

"I can imagine, we never let you interpreters rest. Any insider news?" he said affably.

"No, just the usual—endless bickering. NATO caused some fights."

"Because of Clinton—he's focused on reelection."

"Yes. And the halls were buzzing with the Likud victory."

"Definitely a turn for the worse."

While they chatted, she wondered who was in the apartment with Lawrence, for she could hear male voices through the wall. She discreetly rang the bell to give Lawrence warning while simultaneously rummaging in her purse for her key. Then she took more time fumbling with the lock. Finally, as the lock gave, she turned back with a pretty smile for the ambassador. "Tell me what you need, Max." She stepped into the hallway, and thankfully the voices from the bedroom had quieted.

"Well, it's quite embarrassing," the ambassador said, coming in and looking at his watch. "I'm supposed to meet the pope's plane in an hour, and I'm locked out of our apartment. Sandra's still at our friends' barbecue in Fiano, and it's our maid's day off, so I can't get in."

"Yikes," Antonella laughed, eyeing his clothes. "I guess you can't meet the pope looking like that. Why's he so late?"

"He's coming from Hawaii. I thought perhaps Lawrence could lend me a suit. And of course I'll have it cleaned before I return it."

"No worries, but you're so tall, Ambassador, and what about shoes? Lawrence is size ten."

"I'm eleven, I'll manage."

"Could you wait here a sec?" She gave his arm a reassuring pat and then opened the door to the suite, slipped inside, and closed it.

Gene was standing in the bedroom, stark naked, and Lawrence was on the other side of the bed, tossing him a plastic bag, from which clothes tumbled out on the bed.

"What's going on in here? For Christ's sake!" Antonella hissed. "Ambassador Wagner's out there! He needs immediate help. Gene, get the fuck in the study!"

"It was an emergency—I had to sleep. If I didn't, it would be like Steely Dan says—'die behind the wheel.'" He chortled as he staggered down the little hall with Antonella pushing his naked back.

"And be quiet!" she whispered.

He stumbled into the study and she closed the door fast, but at the last minute reached her hand back in to flick on the light.

Lawrence was in the hallway looking helpless.

Antonella glared at him and grabbed the plastic bag from his hands. "What the fuck, Larry!"

"It's not what you think!"

"Hurry, the ambassador's out there—he needs to borrow your clothes."

She went back to the study and tossed the plastic bag into it. But in opening the door she was horrified to see the neighbors' dinner party on the balcony next door. Everyone—including Natalie—was looking through the picture window at Gene, who crouched behind Lawrence's treadmill, hardly concealed. "Serves you right!" she hissed and switched off the light. She heard his snarl as she closed the door.

At the other end of the hall, she could hear Lawrence giving the ambassador a tour of his suits in the bedroom closet. She listened for a second to Lawrence's English, enunciated so precisely, but still sounding just like Italian music.

"Do you want to try on a few?—see how they fit? And you're much taller than I."

"When do you find time to wear all these? My Italian doctors wear jeans."

"So do I, though pressed, of course. But the older doctors still dress up. And every now and then I go to a conference, or a funeral, and wear a suit. Hey, I've worn a suit to your parties. But generally, I've never worn most of these. My mother likes to shop for good buys."

"I'd love a mother like that—I have to wear a suit every day. I guess we Austrians still like our uniforms." He laughed. "I'll try this one. Maybe the pinstripes will catch more attention than the hemline."

"Good idea. And it's double-breasted, super retro—people will stare at the jacket and not the pants."

"I apologize for interrupting Antonella's homecoming. Mmm … she's some dish, isn't she?"

"I wouldn't let her hear you say that."

"Oh? Not PC?"

"Come on, you know that, Max."

The ambassador chuckled. "Okay, I'll do better, though I'm still old school. Which reminds me, I saw your sister on television the other day. She really socks it to you—and damn, she gets into incredibly personal stuff."

"Personal but human—pretty universal, if you ask me."

Just then the phone rang, startling Antonella in the hall-way.

"I'll get it, Larry," she called out, running for the kitchen phone, pretty sure who the caller was and not wanting the ambassador to be privy to the conversation. Indeed, it was Natalie.

"What's going on over there?"

"I don't know, I just walked in from Brussels, and…"

"Gene is stark naked—we saw *everything* from our balcony, I mean *everything*—Michelangelo's *Moses*, without the drapery!"

Antonella laughed. "Good one. But I'll have to call you tomorrow. Ambassador Wagner's here. He's locked out and needs to borrow a suit to meet the pope at the airport."

"Your house is crazy! I can't believe you're rekindling that perverse affair."

"Obviously I'm not, Natalie. I just got home. And what-ever's going on with Gene and Lawrence, it wouldn't have happened if I had just stayed single. Men create messes and women have to clean them up."

"Don't blame me. I've always told you men are less evolved. But we love them anyway, so it's what it is. And Lawrence adores you—that's all that counts. If you have expectations, you'll always feel let down. So, go with the flow, that's my motto."

"Because you're divorced and safe."

Natalie sighed. "Just try to remember you have a good husband who'll be an excellent father. I hope you're working on that."

"I hope you're done with lectures."

"Advice, free advice. I've lived longer. Call me tomorrow."

Antonella hung up and joined Lawrence and the ambassador by the front door. They were chuckling, and Antonella smiled too when she saw the ambassador's trouser cuffs a good four inches above his Top-Siders. He carried a pair of Lawrence's dress shoes in his hand, planning to squeeze into them at the last minute. His toothy grin wagged at her. "My driver's waiting. I thank you both for saving me, and I'm sorry for all the trouble. If it weren't the pope, I would've called my deputy."

"But it's the pope," they chorused together, and then the ambassador left.

Lawrence looked at Antonella with imploring eyes and a helpless shrug of his shoulders. She glared back, but before she could speak, the bedroom door swung open and Gene came out dressed in his smelly clothes.

"Some rest, but it sure woke me up," he said. He opened the front door and looked back at them. "Thanks, and I'm sorry, Antonella. I guess I'm sorry, Lar. See you around." He left, not wanting to linger a moment longer.

Lawrence turned and tried to put his arms around

Antonella. "*Amore…*"

"Don't '*amore*' me."

She headed to the kitchen and he followed.

"I'm so happy you're home. Welcome home. That jerk just barged in. I couldn't get rid of him. And then, I stopped trying. He had fallen asleep at the wheel."

She flung up her arms in exasperation. "You don't know what it feels like! I'm so sick of the world and stupid men. Brussels—90 percent egocentric chauvinists—my taxi driver a total pervert, Max calling me 'a dish,' and then you, you and Gene doing who knows what in my own home, my own bedroom."

"We weren't doing anything. I hate the guy. He forced himself in and stank like a pisshole. I couldn't stop him from helping himself to the shower, and then he conked out."

Antonella listened with pursed lips, her anger still strong. But she knew Gene and could imagine the scenario Lawrence had described. He saw his advantage and went on.

"I realized, much as I hate his guts, he was a person, and I didn't want to send him back on the road if it caused a crash."

Antonella nodded, her anger subsiding. A tiny smile touched the corners of her lips. Their brown eyes met, hers lighter than his, his like dark velvet and deeply set with long lashes. "Okay, I smell artichokes."

They grinned at each other, and he hugged her. "Welcome home, Mamma made the artichokes just for you. I want to hear all about your trip, right from the beginning. Shall we eat outside?"

Their dinner proceeded in a happier mood. They sat next

to each other on the terrace couch and ate all of the artichokes. They talked and laughed with their usual ease and comaraderie.

Rome's light, fragrant air permeated the verdant compound, carrying the heady scent of *Pittosporum* on its soft breeze. A few dinner parties continued to ripple from neighboring balconies, sheltered by awnings. Rome's long-lasting evening scintillated. Enjoyment filled the atmosphere from the city's encircling hills to its tiniest, hidden piazzas in the very heart of the ancient labyrinth. There, the sound of running water could always be heard, mixing with the odor of history, of ghostly lives, seeping from the grimy stones.

Even after they finished eating, they lingered longer just to nestle close to each other in the beautiful spring night. Finally, Antonella stirred and began clearing their plates from the coffee table. "I'm bushed."

Lawrence got up and helped. "I'll clean up. You can unpack," he said.

"Thanks, luv, I'll take you up on that," she said.

"I love it when you call me luv," he said, smiling at her, his hands holding the empty artichoke pan.

She kissed his cheek and whispered sexily in his ear, "Luv."

He laughed, delighted.

In the bedroom, as she unpacked, she could hear Lawrence singing while he cleaned up the kitchen. He had the radio on and was belting out a Franco Battiato song full throttle, loving to hit the high notes, his special talent. She smiled, loving to hear him sing, it was always so carefree and happy. His positive mood did so much for her, as if she could hide something of herself, something introspective and less cheerful, behind it.

Lawrence was just coming into the bedroom suite when the outside doorbell rang. They exchanged a surprised look—it was late, ten o'clock. They went to the intercom, and Lawrence spoke into its microphone, "*Chi è?*"

"Lawrence, hi, it's me, Jenny. Sorry it's so late. I couldn't find a phone to call first."

"Mamma," Antonella said, as Lawrence pressed the button that released the front gate.

"Toni, I won't keep you, but wanted to give you some news, preferably in person."

"Come on in, we're on the second floor."

While they waited for her at the open front door, Antonella said, "News in person isn't good news."

Jenny stepped out of the elevator, carrying a large, quilted bag. She was almost seventy but looked younger, perhaps because she wore jeans and a T-shirt under a light blue jacket. Her gray hair was pulled back in a ponytail, with wispy bangs across her forehead. They hugged and kissed, and then Jenny peered curiously at Lawrence.

"Was that you singing? I could hear someone."

"Must have been me, yeah, the kitchen window's open— guess I gave the neighborhood a free concert." He grinned, as they moved to the living room.

"I didn't know you could sing."

"You've met him only once," Antonella said, "at the civic part of our wedding."

"Yes, I know. That was Rosini's fault. You know he can't

stand crowds and is only happy when he's in his lair. But we did invite you for Christmas."

They sat down, Jenny in one of the armchairs and Antonella and Lawrence on the couch facing her.

"Yes, but Christmas is when Lawrence's family goes to the Dolomites. But, Mamma, what's going on … why are you in Rome? Is everything all right?"

"Well, not exactly, and first of all, I apologize for not calling earlier, but I wasn't sure until twenty minutes ago I'd have time to stop by. And you know I don't have a cell phone, nor does my friend Renata. We attended an all-day breathing workshop not far from here. There was a dinner afterward."

"Are you … is Papa—"

"I have cancer—breast—with spread to the nodes. So I'm going to need treatment."

The news felt like a blow to Antonella's entire body and cut off her breath. The word *cancer* repeated in her head like the tolling bell of death. She felt Lawrence's hand take hers on the couch between them. She heard her own voice come as if from the ceiling on a drift of wind. "Mamma."

"It's okay, sweetie. I'm still here, and I'm dealing with this. "

"Can you stay with us tonight? You're not driving home, are you?"

"I'm staying with Renata, heading home in the morning."

"Why not with us?"

"It just worked out this way—we took the workshop together…" Her voice trailed off lamely, and Lawrence's hand gave Antonella's a supportive squeeze.

She felt bitter and angry inside, an old hurt, for here was

her mother, the same as she had always been, handing over deeply personal family news like a mail lady delivering an ordinary letter. Why wasn't her mother's heart connecting to her in this moment? Why had it never connected, no matter how much Antonella yearned and reached out for it? Though, by her thirties, she had become more objective, more protective of reigniting her childhood wounds.

Lawrence was keeping the conversation going, while his hand fed her love and support. "Who's your doctor, Jenny? And where are you being treated? Should we get a second opinion? I know the best surgeons and oncologists at Gemeli—and I can follow your case."

Jenny gave a hoarse laugh. "Rome? If I did anything here, it would be in Milan, but I'm going home, to California—Mill Valley, to be exact."

"So far away? Don't you want to be near us?" Antonella said.

"It's okay, sweetie. We both know, and Lawrence knows too, that I have the best chance in the States. I've been in touch with an old college friend, Steve Nelson. He's got a healing center based on ancient dream incubation, and I'm going to try it. I'll be a resident there for six months."

"You mean no Western medicine at all? No chemo or radiation?" Lawrence asked.

"You had spread, Mamma."

"I know, and I might have to do it, but for now, they've taken the tumor, and I want to try Steve's methods first. If an MRI shows something in six months, then I'll consider the other treatments. Steve works with great MDs in San Fran."

"Couldn't we get another opinion here first?" Lawrence said.

"No, but thanks, dear, I really appreciate it. I'm all set, I know what I want to do."

"What're Steve's methods?" Antonella said.

Jenny briefly described Steve's work in dream incubation. He had begun as a Jungian psychologist, and that led to a sideline interest in alchemy. He had spent time with a French doctor who had left Western medicine and revived the ancient healing methods of the Phôlarchos—the Greek and Roman healers who were the priests of Apollo. In those pre-Platonic days, before Western approaches to life and medicine, a sick person would lie perfectly still in a cave until he or she entered a state of altered consciousness—pure awareness—like the state of meditation. Then, a dream or a vision from the gods, or the individual's divine unconscious, would rise to help heal the area of illness, whether physical or mental. The Phôlarchos guided the process, being the divine medium.

"Steve's been helping patients for twenty years, and of course he's added all kinds of other alternative practices to his work. A tech magnate he cured funded his new center. He's also written a book," Jenny said, "and I'm sure he'd love it if you translated it, Toni. He wants to get his work known in Europe—we aren't getting any younger."

Antonella sighed, her head slightly shaking. "So much to take in, Mamma. I wish you were staying. California's so far."

"Don't worry," Jenny said, "I feel optimistic, and we'll stay in touch."

"What does Papa say?"

"Ha! Rosini said, 'If you want caves, we have them right here in Italy. In fact, we have the original one of Parmenides.'" She laughed. "Just like him, more absorbed in his work than anything else."

The words brought up an instant image in Antonella's mind. She saw her father standing in the open French doors to his study, like a towering wizard with a graying beard and wild, frizzy hair—the hair she had inherited, but hers a shade of red. His coal-black eyes shone at her from across the villa's tiled front lobby, where, as a little girl, she played by herself on the floor. She stared back at him in awe. His whole face glowed—a white radiance beamed off of him. He didn't look earthly, he looked like a being from an unknown planet. He didn't speak, he just stared at her with those laser-beaming eyes. Then he stepped back into his study and closed the doors. Only later, during college, had it occurred to her that if she had been a son, he would have whisked her into his life and secret knowledge from birth. He would have passed on his soul and passion to her. And she would have known his touch instead of longing for it. His touch. She had craved it, but felt it only those times when she was sick. Like during one of their weekend drives through Umbria and Toscana on the hunt for rare plants. She was four or five, and the winding roads made her horribly carsick in the back seat of their old Fiat station wagon, its back area filling with bundles of weedy stalks. Her father drove with a hunter's focus, and her mother sat in the passenger seat reading a Buddhist magazine. Antonella's carsickness would become so acute that eventually

Rosini would pull over and park. Reaching over Jenny, who never stopped reading, he'd take a phial of his peppermint remedy from the glove box and climb into the tight back seat with Antonella. How she loved those moments of his great godly form hovering over her, his large, sculpted hand lifting her head as he carefully shook the bottle's hot, stinging drops onto her tongue, instantly cutting the nausea. How she longed to reach up and put her arms around his neck and feel cradled in his arms. She never turned down a trip, despite the agony of her nausea, for those long hours with her parents were rare.

Jenny was going on in a bantering way about how Rosini couldn't be parted from his lab, where he experimented. He entrusted production at his plant, ten miles away, to his disciples, with Jenny overseeing the business end.

"Oh yes, Antonella has told me all about his work, and we take his potions every day—I feel optimum health!" Lawrence gave a champion's raised fist.

"Yeah, which doesn't explain why I got cancer. Rosini's really scratching his head over that."

"Is Papa going to California too?"

"Nope, and I wouldn't want him there. Are you kidding? He'd be restless the whole time and condescending to Steve. He'd find everything wrong with Steve's scholarship and interpretation. And the pasta wouldn't taste like Italy's. I'd end up worrying about him instead of myself. That's probably why I got cancer—the stress of Rosini." She gave a dry laugh, then got up, her mission accomplished. "I hate to make this so short, but Renata's waiting for me downstairs. I'll call when I know more." She smiled at them as they stood up to accompany her to the door. "It's good to see the two of you—you're a good-looking couple." She turned to Lawrence. "She takes after her father's side, if you haven't noticed." Then she laughed and muttered, "Rosini."

At the door, Antonella again felt the speed of her mother's visit—a mere drive-by to deliver life-and-death news to her daughter, as if sharing the news were less important to her than attending a breathing workshop, eating dinner with the other New Agers, and spending the night with one of them instead of with her family—supposedly where love in its deepest form existed. But this was the way Jenny had always been. She and Antonella had never shared that kind of deep love. Lawrence was the closest she had ever come to feeling it.

After the elevator took Jenny away, Lawrence put his arms around Antonella. "What an evening," he said softly.

She pressed her nose to his neck, and he held her, feeling her desire to cave in and cry. "I know," he said against her hair, near her ear. And he did know. He understood the old pain Jenny's visit had reawakened in her—a pain begun in childhood that she had sealed off so as not to feel it. He knew it wasn't the cancer news that upset her as much as Jenny's complete lack of connection to her, to them, despite her outward ease and familiarity—love by the book. She hadn't glanced at their home, which she had never seen, nor had she asked a single question about their lives. She commented on their good looks, that was all.

"Come on, *amore,* let's turn in. We need to *incubate,* big time," Lawrence said.

Antonella laughed. "Good one." Then she paused and

looked into his eyes. She smiled, her eyes so unusually warm. "I love you, Larry."

He gave a jolt of surprise and pleasure. It made her realize how rarely, if ever, she told him that. In fact, unconsciously she related to him with a subtle protection against love, against the natural connection that came so easily to him. It was her "shield" that Natalie had warned her about many times. Jenny's visit had opened her eyes to why she protected herself—she had grown up in an environment of privileged safety but without the bond of love. A surge of motivation filled her to end that legacy of resistance to love, to true relationship. Synchronously, the old peasant woman from her dream the year before rose in her mind. She saw the two gold coins in her palm. It all made sense now—she wanted to be a mother, she wanted to love and nurture children, experience their lives, be a family with Lawrence.

Lawrence watched the array of feelings crossing Antonella's face. He wondered what she was thinking. And now, her gold-brown eyes and Madonna sweetness landed on him with a loving glow. A thrill shot through him. He knew what it meant even before she tugged his sleeve and said, "Let's make love, *tesoro.*"

The Wagners' Party
(2001)

It was an early June evening, and Antonella was playing a game on the den rug with her three-year-old twins, Rita and Angelo. The game's square cards were laid out like a checkerboard, and the children's little hands turned them over, trying to match the colorful images of animals, insects, and fruit. Each time they made a match they squealed with delight, and Antonella squealed too when she made a match. She loved spending time with the kids—indoors, outdoors, and with other children and parents. She had left her full-time job at the ministry and now freelanced. When she had to attend a world summit, Lawrence's mother gladly took care of the children. Lawrence, who still had so much "boy" in him, was a wonderful playmate for the twins when home from work. Overall, Antonella felt a satisfying balance in her life, with time for both motherhood and her own pursuits, which included translating books. She had joined a group of English and American translators, and once a month they met to discuss their projects. Hers was Steve Nelson's book on dream incubation. Jenny was still living at his healing center in California. Her cancer was in remission, but she was continuing her healing work while helping Steve run the center's programs. It seemed a déjà vu of her past devotion to Rosini's career. On the other hand, she had been a seeker of healing arts all her life.

"Your turn, Mamma!" the kids clamored.

Antonella laughed and randomly flipped two cards sitting next to each other that didn't match.

"Dummy," Rita said and made an instant match with one of the cards Antonella had turned over. Then her nimble fingers flipped more cards, making matches that made her snort with pride while her brother scowled.

Antonella wished her mother could see them, know them, love them the way Lawrence's parents did. But occasional phone calls had been their main connection, with one visit to California the summer before. It was easier to be in touch with Rosini, and Umbria was a nice escape from the city. The old wizard stayed mostly in his study or lab, but the kids didn't mind—they were happiest roaming the vast outdoors with their parents and Rosini's black labs, Osiris and Isis. The undulating countryside, with crisscrossing white roads without end, fed their natural exuberance. Back in the villa, they loved sitting in the old-fashioned kitchen with Maria the cook, who fed them snacks while telling stories about her family. Rosini's realm was one of novelty and enchantment for the kids. They didn't need the old alchemist. It was only Antonella who wished he needed them. During their last visit, seated around the rustic table for dinner, she had asked her father, "Do you ever ask Mamma if she's coming back?"

Rosini had shrugged. "*Boh.*"

"What do you mean, '*boh*,' Papa?"

"I mean she has to do what's right for her."

"But don't you want to know if she's coming back?"

His eyes glowed with their extraterrestrial peculiarity. "Jenny's a nomad. I'm amazed she lasted here forty years." He returned to eating his pasta, adding without looking up, "Life's a journey. Each of us has to find our own way."

Suddenly, the children jumped up from the memory game and scampered out of the den. Loud noises were coming from the Wagners' garden below—hammering and workmen's shouts. Antonella followed the children to the living-room balcony, where they leaned over the low brick wall to see what was going on. The Wagners were having their annual spring party that night, and Antonella and Lawrence were planning to go, but only briefly, for it was also Lawrence's forty-third birthday, and the Gaspari clan was coming for dinner—Natalie too, for she would also be at the Wagners. Woody, though, was in the States looking for investors—he and Gene were making movies.

Preparation for the Wagners' party had been going on all week, and now the finishing touches were being installed— tall torches being hammered into the ground and enormous wicker thrones carried by workmen down the concrete ramp that connected the Wagners' first-floor apartment to their garden. Sandra Wagner was out there waving her arms and shouting about the chairs.

"Put them there, two in front of the oleander and three next to the palm trees! Dino! Get out of the way!" Her five-year-old son was kicking his soccer ball down the ramp, tangling up in the legs of the delivery men.

"Dino!" Angelo cried out from the balcony. "Let's play!"

"It's not a good time, honey," Antonella said, "Sandra's getting ready for her party."

"But Dino's playing!"

"Yes, but it's his garden." She glanced at her watch. "Your *nonni* will be here any minute—maybe they'll take you to the playground."

"Yes!" the children chimed, jumping up and down in excitement, "The playground!"

Antonella smiled at their cherubic faces, so full of innocent delight. "And let's remember to sing 'Happy Birthday' when Papa comes in," she said.

They skipped inside, clapping and crowing, "Happy birthday! Happy birthday, Papa!" They picked up their toy-sized scooters and zipped around the spacious hardwood floor, stunning Antonella with their dexterity.

"I'm going to get dressed for the party," she told them. "Please stay inside."

She went to her closet to find something to wear to the party. It would be a high-fashion affair at the Wagners', the guests wearing the season's latest. Her fingers moved through a row of beautiful dresses, but all of them from the past—her past of official events with the ministry and the EU. Finally, she chose a satiny dress that reminded her of a Klimt painting with its shimmering gold and purple pattern. Her coppery hair would go well with the colors, adding more glitter. She laughed to herself. But who was she dressing up for? Men? Since marriage, men ignored her—her wedding band set an immediate barrier, even for a short, enjoyable conversation. They saw her ring and discarded her as an option, meaning she and other women were only worthwhile as sexual objects. Before marriage, men flocked around her, and after marriage, she was nothing.

The phone rang. It was Sandra from downstairs. "Darling," she said in her high-strung voice, "things are *impazzite* down here! And guests are about to arrive—I still have to dress, *Dio mio*! We have ambassadors coming and a cardinal. And Zanetti!" He was a past president. "Everything has to be perfect. And I know Angelo thinks I'm being mean because I didn't allow playdates this week, but it's the only way I can handle such complicated preparations."

"Of course."

"And I'm calling to ask if you could please tell Angelo to stop throwing his LEGO into my garden."

"Oh, I'm so sorry, yes, right away!"

"Thank you, darling, and Boris will bring up the toys." Boris was their Russian chauffeur.

Antonella hurried to the balcony, where the kids stood on tiptoes at the wall, Angelo shooting LEGO pieces at targets. "*Bambini*! Come inside! No balconies without an adult! Angelo, you can't throw LEGO into the Wagners' yard. Everything will be back to normal tomorrow, but today we have to be extra respectful. This is Sandra's important party." Antonella looked over the wall and saw workmen rolling synthetic green turf down the garden's ramp. "*Mamma mia!*" she laughed.

"Why are they putting grass on the bridge?" Rita asked.

"I have no idea, *tesoro*, and it's fake. Come on, let's go in. I need to shower and dress, *nonni* will be here in a minute."

"But I want my LEGO," Angelo said.

"Don't worry, Sandra's sending it up."

The doorbell rang, and it was Alma and Stan, their arms carrying provisions for the birthday party—Stan a bakery box with the cake and Alma, a lasagna pan covered with a cloth. Stan's toe touched a baggie by the threshold. "Look here," he said.

Angelo pounced on the bag. "My LEGO!"

Amid busy greetings, Antonella took the lasagna pan from Alma, and Stan put the cake box on the hall table. Everyone hugged and kissed while talking at once. Stan was tall and bony, and although white-haired and wizened, he looked younger than his early seventies. So did Alma with her trim figure and former beauty still visible, especially in its legacy to Lawrence. The kids began tugging at their grandparents' clothes, chanting to go to the playground.

"*Si, certo, tesori, andiamo.* Get your shoes!" Alma said, mixing Italian and English. To Antonella she said, "Where's our birthday boy?"

"Probably on his way home. I'll give him a call. And thanks for all the food, *genitori!* Mmm, the lasagna smells so good! We'll only stay a minute at the party."

"Take your time, enjoy yourselves," Alma said. "I'll feed the kids after the playground."

The children dropped their sneakers by the adults, who

crouched down to help put them on. Sweatshirts followed, for the sun was going down, with cooler air wafting in through the open terrace doors. June was one of Rome's loveliest months, before the summer heat set in. The little park and playground across the street from the condominium gates would be full of children and parents before dinnertime at eight. The park's kiosk would be bustling with business, everyone wanting snacks, coffee, and gelato. Stan picked up the kids' scooters, and with a round of goodbyes, the entourage set off, squeezing into the narrow elevator.

Antonella watched them go from the door, a fond smile on her lips. How lucky to enjoy such simple moments together, she thought. That was what she had gained by joining the Rowinski-Gaspari family. Closing the door and returning to her room to get ready for the party, she couldn't help but compare life with the Gasparis to life at the Rosinis. Her parents had little curiosity about other people, and Rosini never questioned a man's superiority and entitlement.

At that same recent dinner at the villa, the kids were giggling over the dogs nudging them for scraps from the table. Rosini had turned to Angelo with a conspiratorial wink and passed him a morsel from his plate. Angelo took it and gingerly, with a fearful face, dropped it into Osiris's chomping jaws, retracting his hand fast. Rosini had laughed and tousled the boy's dark curly hair that came from his own genes. Then he invited Angelo for a tour of the lab, describing its big tanks, gushing tubes, and blazing ovens as if they were an adventure that couldn't be missed. Not once did he look at Rita or include her in his invitation, and Antonella filled with a familiar anger. "Papa, Rita would like to see the lab too."

Rosini's radiance had instantly dimmed, but in the end all four of them took the tour, and whenever Rosini picked up Angelo to explain a process taking place in one of the segments of loud machinery, Lawrence had picked up Rita and repeated the information.

Antonella felt grateful for Lawrence. Their marriage was good. They loved and respected each other, even though passion had faded and lovemaking had become hardly exciting. The permanency of marriage, the knowledge that desire and stimulation with a man—fresh, inspiring love—were no longer going to happen to her—ever—sometimes filled her with longing for the freedom to fall in love again. She felt it most when she traveled for work and was part of a scene with well-dressed and handsome men. Who were they? She wanted to find out, mix and discover, be discovered herself, be desired. Yes, it was all ego, but sexual ego existed.

Antonella showered and dressed, but Lawrence still wasn't home. She decided to go without him. She called his cell phone one last time and left a message to meet her at the Wagners'. Then it occurred to her to try his office line. Often he had last-minute walk-ins, patients with a fever or injury that he couldn't turn away. He surprised her by picking up, his voice weirdly groggy. "Uh, *cazzo*! The party—I'm late!"

A woman's mew sounded right after he spoke, as if someone were nuzzling his neck. All too quickly, unnaturally, he said, "See you soon, *amore*, and give the kids a kiss for me." He clicked off, and Antonella stood there feeling a rush of horror and disbelief. Who had mewed? Was it his new receptionist, Fiamma? She was in her twenties and quite pretty with long dark hair and a voluptuous figure that her clingy clothes accentuated. Antonella had met her and right away wondered how Lawrence and the other male doctors in the practice could resist noticing her, even fantasizing about her, when her body and pretty face posed before their eyes all day long.

Bad feelings churned in her as she took the stairs down to the Wagners' apartment. Her mind was full of images of what was going on and how she would deal with Lawrence when he got home. And it was his birthday! Was he giving himself a middle-age birthday treat? How disgusting! And she now faced two parties that would last until ten o'clock before she could confront him. But maybe nothing had actually happened. Oh, wishful thinking! She had heard his flustered voice and a woman's kittenish cooing. They had just had sex! She wasn't naive.

Ambassador Wagner's toothy grin greeted Antonella at the door. She smiled and they exchanged kisses. Both the ambassador and his wife—Sandra was across the room—wore the buff-colored summer suits she had seen displayed in all the windows along via Condotti.

"Antonella, welcome, come in, I'm so glad you could come. Where's Lawrence?"

"On his way."

"Doctors' hours. Follow me, I want you to try my punch," Max said, putting his arm around her waist like an old lover and leading her to the bar. "I learned the recipe from my American girlfriend during my UN days."

The server ladled the pale pink drink into a punch cup and with pincers, dropped a slice of kiwi into it.

"Oh, why Prince and Princess!" Max said, turning away from Antonella to bow graciously over the hands of new arrivals. "Sandra and I are honored to have you join us this evening! Will you try some of my famous American punch?"

The prince was a balding man with no expression on his bland face, and the blonde princess, still in her twenties, looked like an ornament to his lapel, a white carnation or a crimson pocket square. Antonella was familiar with this social set from her ministry work, where the women who accompanied the male dignitaries were either their tenacious wives, or their new, young trinkets. Once, at a diplomatic dinner, she had been seated between two male envoys—a German and a Brit. At first they spoke politics, leaning forward to bypass her. Then they rocked back on their chairs to continue the conversation behind her back. She had felt furious—she knew the political news as well as they and could converse equally on the topic—or on any topic in their mutual foreign affairs field. But in their world, women attended such dinners only as ornaments to the men. A few female diplomats were also present, but either single or attending without their husbands, who tagged along in their own invisible careers and were rarely seen. Unlike diplomats' wives, diplomats' husbands had no role in their spouse's career.

Antonella stepped away from the bar and noticed Natalie coming in the door on the arm of an elderly, military officer with medals on his uniform. Natalie's petite figure wore the season's buff-colored suit, the skirt as short as she dared, and her purse, shoes, scarf, and jewelry all selected to match. Her hair gleamed, not one strand loose from the whole, as if the hair had come out of a mold in solid form. Although her glamour was intact, Natalie immediately stepped away from her escort to check her appearance in the little hallway that had a wall mirror. It was the same hallway and mirror in Antonella's apartment on the floor above.

Antonella wove through the growing throng to join Natalie in front of the mirror, where the older woman was reapplying red lipstick. Meeting Antonella's eyes in the silvery sheen, Natalie said, "Darling, I'm just freshening up before I meet all those VIPs. I heard Zanetti's coming, is it true?" She rubbed her lips together and gave Antonella's reflection a smile. "How do I look?"

"Fabulous, but you've got lipstick on your front teeth."

"Eek, what if you weren't here? This is what happens in old age! Be forewarned!" She wiped the red from her teeth and smiled again.

"Better. It's gone."

"Good. Did you see my general?"

"I did, who is he?"

"General Borroni, long retired, of course. But at one time high up in the Defense Ministry. We're flirting while Woody's away, it's so much fun."

"I'm jealous, marriage is so dull," Antonella said with a smile.

"I know. And it's fun when old acquaintances pop out of the woodwork—free flirting." She took hold of Antonella's arm for better balance in her heels as they wove through the guests toward the bar. "You look so pretty tonight. What a beautiful dress—the gold reminds me of Klimt."

"Me too—that's why I bought it, years ago."

"Well, its beauty is timeless. Shall we go outside?"

"Yes, less crowded."

They picked up a glass of punch for Natalie and stepped out on the ramp to the garden. It was a perfect spring night, the air redolent of tender blossoms and lush greenery. Rome's light breeze traveled through the deep blue sky of sunset's aftermath that left violet streaks across the horizon. The jazz band's music at the far end of the garden was mellow, allowing conversation to flow at a natural volume.

Natalie tapped the toe of her two-toned party shoe with its dainty strap on the carpeted ramp. "I feel like the guest of royalty."

"That's what they want. You should have seen how much work went into this party. They put down the fake grass an hour ago."

"My, my, what some people spend their time thinking about. Where's your husband? I'm looking forward to his birthday party."

"And your general's welcome too, I didn't know you were coming with someone."

"No, no, I'm leaving with you. He knows. I just needed an escort to arrive with—someone distinguished." She chuckled.

The garden looked lovely, its walls coated in pink oleander, with several tall, leaning umbrella pines gracing the lawn with their regal stature. Scattered urns with hydrangea and other flowering plants added to the luxuriant setting. Tall torches would soon be lit, completing the idyllic atmosphere.

An older woman in a red dress and heavy makeup came out on the ramp and lit a cigarette that immediately set off a coughing attack.

"Why, Carmela," Natalie said, greeting the woman in red. "I'm surprised to see you in Rome. This is my friend and colleague from the ministry, Antonella Rosini Gaspari."

The two women nodded politely, and then all three continued down the ramp to the garden.

"Yes, I'm in Rome these days, gladly. I'm done with globe-trotting just to repair our properties. I'm not getting any younger." She took another drag on her cigarette and coughed with thick congestion that sounded suffocating. Even so, between sputters, she tried to keep the conversation going. "Today, our butler in Acapulco called to say one of the bathrooms was out of order. I told him, 'Then there are still eight that work!'"

They had reached the garden, where Carmela dropped her half-smoked cigarette in the grass and stepped on it. "Well, I think I'll circulate a bit." She smiled with brown, decayed teeth. "Nice seeing you, Natalie, and meeting you, signora." She coughed as she left them, clearing her vocal channels for her next conversation.

"Adieu!" Antonella hissed to Natalie.

"You're not kidding," Natalie agreed.

"Ciao, Mamma," a conspiratorial voice came down from the upper balcony. Antonella looked up and found the beaming faces of Angelo and Rita, surrounded by ferns and palm fronds. Then she noticed Alma a few feet behind them, smiling like an indulgent governess.

"*Bambini*! How was the playground? Are you spying on us?"

"I had gelato, three flavors: *limone, fragola, e cioccolato.*"

"*Anch'io,*" Rita said.

"And the *nonni*?"

"They didn't want gelato. Nonno had a caffè."

"I'll be home soon, darlings! I love you!" She blew them a kiss.

The children laughed, blew kisses back, and pattered off with Alma waving goodbye.

Seeing the family reminded Antonella of Lawrence and the shock of his office romance. As she and Natalie took seats in two of the wicker thrones, she said, "Lawrence is fooling around with his new receptionist."

"Good God! I really hoped he might be different. Unfortunately, lust is coded into men's behavior."

"Women's too."

"Yes, but don't you think we add in other criteria?"

"Yes, but not always."

"Well, at least the Italian men I've known don't leave their wives and family when they stray for sex."

"What are you saying? It's not about whether *he* leaves or not. It's about whether I let him stay!"

"Men have always sought mistresses. They serve a man's ego—juggling two women at once—you, his dependable, unsuspecting, and beloved wife, and the pretty young thing who's there just for sex." She sipped her drink.

"Adrienne Rich says, 'it's desire without discrimination:

to want a woman like a fix.'"

"Mmm, I like that. His secretary is just an alluring body to him, but for her, he's a handsome, mature doctor—he's God."

Antonella choked on a laugh. "Lawrence is not God."

"To her, he is. How did you find out?"

"I phoned him and heard her purring in the background, like right on his neck."

Natalie settled back and drew a breath, preparing for one of her long speeches that Antonella knew only too well.

"Well, offices have always been havens for affairs, we both know it. Attraction's inevitable. But the poor girl. She's inexperienced, full of hope. She worships her boss and wants nothing more than to selflessly give herself to him, please him. But soon, his blind lust will die out. He's never loved her. But she, on the other hand, is head over heels in love and dreams of marriage, a home together, and babies. When she realizes he doesn't want this, she'll begin to feel shortchanged, resentful. She's given so much, while he only takes. She'll play back all of their encounters and realize they've never been public, never part of the real world. She'll realize he never had any interest in her besides sex in the office. They'll start arguing. He'll feel alarmed that she might stop taking the pill, or worse, telephone you! She'll begin to play the martyred woman, cry at her desk, phone girlfriends—maybe her mother—and cry over her betrayal. He'll get alarmed—patients in the waiting room might hear his name mentioned. Or his fellow doctors in the practice!"

"And it's clearly sexual harassment. It ends with her losing her job, a decent one for a high-school graduate. And she'll be scarred for life in her relationships with men."

"She'll never trust them again. She'll always be angry, wounded, and defensive."

"It's always women who pay the price for male behavior, which is why I never wanted to get married. The altar is where we're sacrificed."

"Hmm, I like that metaphor. But would you give up having Rita and Angelo to be safe and single again?

"No. They're the best thing I've ever known."

"So, since you, and other women, are powerless to change what exists not only in nature but also by unfair tradition and law—patriarchy—I urge you to go on with your own life and profit from your talents. And by all means, lust when you feel like it."

"I can't live a fake life like that. And I don't want to see the jerk every day and pretend it's all okay again," Antonella said.

"Give it time."

"Natalie!"

"Try to let it go."

"No! You're coming from the 1940s, and things have changed. Women are not inferior, we are not chattels to men anymore!"

"It hasn't changed that much—especially when it comes to love, sex, and men. I've witnessed a lifetime of friends suffering because of their husbands' infidelities. And the ones who have suffered the most are the ones who left their husbands. If they had accepted what happened and gone on with their lives, their own pursuits—including lovers of their own—they would have been much happier. But alone, they lost economic support and social standing."

Natalie sipped her drink and noticed Lawrence stepping onto the ramp. "Uh-oh, he's here."

Antonella looked at the ramp and scrutinized her husband objectively—a very good-looking man, freshly showered and chic in a perfectly fitted summer suit—open collar, no tie. His dark hair glistened, the temples sprinkled with gray, his face cleanly shaven. His soccer-player body— he still played in a league—looked taut and healthy, and his whole presence radiated sex appeal that stirred Antonella's attraction even through her anger. And he had just enjoyed sex with that plump *fanciulla*.

His eyes found them seated on the white thrones, and his brow furrowed. He was afraid of the coming interaction with Antonella. He knew whatever words they exchanged would be phony, forced pleasantries covering undercurrents of bad feelings. He was guilty and had no idea how to undo what was done. He was filled with dread, and the two women in those thrones looked like Olympian judges.

"He knows I know," Antonella said through tight lips.

"Indeed, it's written on his face. And he knows we've been talking about him. Poor man—facing women isn't easy."

"Don't feel sorry for him. He just wrecked our family."

Still on the ramp, Lawrence turned and looked up—the twins were calling to him from the balcony.

"*Bambini!*" he said and blew kisses. "How're my little pumpkins?"

Rita began jumping up and down and chanting, "Happy birthday! Happy birthday!"

Angelo followed her lead, adding to the volume of the chants. Guests in the garden stopped talking, and soon an amused twitter filled the air. Lawrence turned to his audience like a star on the stage and waved an arm at the children. "My kids. I love them!"

"Happy birthday!" the guests called back and then spontaneously began to clap. The jazz band struck up "Happy Birthday," the sax peeling out, and everyone began singing. Lawrence smiled broadly from his perch on the ramp and gave a mock bow when the song ended. Then reality hit him, and he faced finishing his descent to the ladies.

"He's just so lovable," Natalie said. "Look how he won over the guests."

"Would they have indulged a woman like that?"

"No, never. We value men more. They're strong and can do things we can't. That's how the double standard got started—from physical power. On the other hand, we worship women in art more than men."

"Do you really think Titian was worshiping his Venuses?"

"Absolutely. He was showing deep reverence for the beauty and sensuality of his model's body."

"Exactly, her body and its seduction in his imagination—he couldn't care less about what was inside her, who she was. He was painting his fantasy of ravishing her. His mouth was watering. She's a beautiful sex object for all time."

"Oh go on! Then so is *David*."

"Yes, so is *David*. Michelangelo adored him, made unrequited love to his image every night after chiseling. That was his boy-love."

Natalie chuckled, and with Lawrence a yard away, they stopped talking. He came to Natalie's chair first.

"Hello, Lawrence, how are you?"

He took her raised hand and kissed it. He glanced at Antonella and received her stony rejection. He dropped a faint kiss on top of her head and forced some conversation. "How's the party? Those chairs look comfortable, I think I'll grab one."

He left before they could answer, and they watched as he effortlessly lifted a chair over his head from Sandra's other arrangement and carried it back to them.

"See what I mean about strength," Natalie said under her breath.

Lawrence put the chair down so that they formed a triangle. "President Zanetti's here," he said.

"I'll have to shake his hand before I leave," Natalie said. "I was his interpreter several times during his presidency. I wonder if he remembers."

"Max and Sandra are all excited about who's here," Antonella said dryly.

"Many people like to collect other people they think are more important—it boosts their egos," Natalie said.

"It's a boring, *People* magazine world," Antonella said.

"I see you're not enjoying yourself," Lawrence said.

"I have a lot on my mind."

Lawrence looked away and said nothing. If they knew of his transgression, which he felt certain they did after that phone call, then he wasn't going to participate in the conversation's drift, especially with Natalie there.

"Why is it that everyone at this party was born into

privilege, and to such a degree that the world's misery and tragedies never occur to them," Antonella said. "Their only troubling thoughts when they go to bed at night, needing sleeping pills, are how to afford that new thing that will make them look better than their friends."

"I'm sorry you're feeling down right now, but I hate it when you get on your soapbox," Lawrence said. There were a few beats of silence, before he added, "How're the kids? Did they tire you out today?"

"Only the biggest one."

Natalie laughed, but quickly kept the conversation going. "I may live in this world of privilege, but I've never felt a part of it. Having survived two revolutions with my mother, in which we lost everything both times, I've always known the impermanence of material goods and security. I've had to collect pieces of coal that fell off trains in order to heat our small room when we had nothing. That reminds me of an Italian I know—she said she's never been on a city bus, because it's not befitting her status. A person can talk like that only if they've never had to survive hunger and the threat of death. I love beautiful things too, I'm tempted every day, but ultimately we can do perfectly well, in fact, even better, without such things. I have only two fears in life: drowning and destitution."

At that moment, Sandra Wagner rushed across the lawn to them, her tight skirt giving her a wiggly gait and her stiletto heels sinking into the ground every few steps.

"Oh, Lawrence, you looked so adorable up there on the bridge. Happy birthday!" she said.

He stood and they kissed cheeks. Then Sandra smiled at

Natalie and Antonella, while clinging to Lawrence's arm. "The buffet's ready, please come up and help yourselves—it's from Ferlito's, *squisito.*" She turned with a simpering plea to Lawrence. "I hate to ask a favor, darling, but your chair, would you mind putting it back, so my little arrangements look inviting for President Zanetti. He's about to come down to the garden with his dinner, and I want him to have his pick of chairs."

Natalie and Antonella immediately got up so that all of the chairs would be empty for the former president's pick.

"Oh, *grazie mille!*" Sandra said ingratiatingly. "You can't imagine all the work we did this week. I'm exhausted and already thinking about the cleanup tonight and escaping to the country tomorrow to recover. Thank God I have help."

Lawrence carried his chair away.

"This is a lovely party," Natalie said to Sandra as they stepped toward the ramp. "It reminds me of what the columnist Bettina Tocci once wrote. She said a successful party depends on three things: enough people to stimulate conversation, good food to satisfy the guests, and at least one eminent person to give the party an air of importance."

"Ahh," Sandra smiled proudly, then squeezed Lawrence's arm as he rejoined them. "Thank you so much, darling."

"But what if the party's in a village of poor people?" Antonella said.

"Then, perhaps the town butcher is more important than the shoemaker or the seamstress," Natalie said. "You just need that one person who stands out in his or her community."

"And we have him—here he comes! And thank you, signora … uh," Sandra groped for Natalie's name.

"Edwards. Natalie Jablonska Edwards."

They waited at the base of the ramp for the former president, his bodyguards, and a few important friends to finish their carpeted descent. Natalie stepped forward as soon as Zanetti reached the garden and bowed her head decorously, unable to shake his hand for it held his dinner plate. He bowed back.

"President Zanetti, it's an honor to see you again. I was your interpreter at several summits in the eighties."

Again, he bowed his distinguished head. "Thank you, signora, I do indeed remember you. It would be impossible to forget such a dignified woman who served our country with such dedication and excellence."

They smiled with another round of bows before Sandra obsequiously guided the former president to his choice of thrones.

Back in the house, they worked their way to the door, stopping a few times for Natalie to greet familiar faces. Then she kissed her general goodbye, glad to see him ensconced in a lively conversation with a young diplomat. But he detained them a few more minutes, wanting to introduce Natalie to the young man, who had just returned from five years in Ethiopia. Pleasantries followed, including agreement to meet the following week for lunch on via Veneto. "It will be a pleasure," Natalie said to the gentlemen with her glamorous smile.

Finally, they reached the door, but once again were delayed. Sandra called out, "Wait!" and sailed up to them, looking worried. "Are you leaving already? Don't you want to eat? I hope you aren't mad because of the chairs. We have others—

I can get them out. And we're about to light the torches. It took me weeks to find the torches. We had to order them from Paris."

"But I saw them on the Corso yesterday," Natalie said.

"Those aren't as nice."

"Thank you for having us," Antonella said, leaning forward to kiss Sandra goodbye. "We have Lawrence's family upstairs for his birthday."

"Of course, and thank you for stopping by on such an important day." She looked coquettishly at Lawrence. "Might I ask … ?"

"I'm forty-three."

"Incredible. You look fabulous, darling—hardly any gray. I'm ten years younger and have to cover mine," she said with a self-effacing giggle.

"My dear," Natalie purred, "you don't look a day over twenty-two."

"Oh, thank you, signora … uh …"

"Edwards, but 'countess' if you like, it's easier to remember countess."

"What! You're a countess? Wait till Max hears we had another countess at the party."

"May I ask who the other countess is?" Natalie said.

"Cristina Caruso."

"Ah, Cristina." Natalie dropped her voice and leaned into Sandra's left ear. "I'll share a little secret with you, but you mustn't tell anyone. And I doubt Cristina even knows. Long ago, before either of you were born, her future husband was able to purchase his title—he had connections with … well, let's just say the powers that be."

Antonella silently laughed while Lawrence looked away, pretending not to hear. Natalie could be so devilish. With final, effusive goodbyes, the guests left and took the stairs to the floor above.

Alma greeted them at the door, her warm, inclusive smile like a hug of unconditional love. The children, in clean, ironed pajamas, ran from the den to jump all over Lawrence, who easily scooped them up and showered them with affection. The others looked on fondly, even Antonella. Anything to do with the kids made their elders smile with tenderness. Stan came out of the den where he'd been playing a game with the twins, and more greetings ensued. The senior Gasparis needed no introduction to Natalie, who was part of the family. A spontaneous mixture of English and Italian reverberated in the apartment's open, sparsely furnished space.

"Antonella, I was thinking we should serve the cake first, so the children can go to bed," Alma said.

"Yes! Cake! Cake!" the children sang out and then zig-zagged around the room, their arms out like airplane wings.

"They're exhausted," Alma said. "They always go wild before they collapse."

A few minutes later, with everyone gathered in the dining room, Alma brought out the cake with its twinkling candles. They sang to Lawrence, the children loudly and off-key. Lawrence leaned down, made a wish, and blew out the candles in a single breath. His eyes came up and met Antonella's. He had wished for her forgiveness, and she had thought he might be wishing for that, or that he was in a bad dream and wished to wake up. It wasn't going to be easy to go through the motions of a gay family celebration with so much turmoil broiling between them.

After the kids were tucked into bed, the family went back to the dining room for dinner.

"I don't know what happened to Donna and Matteo," Alma said, "but let's start without them. We're all hungry."

"Starved," Stan said. "And try the TV news if you want to find out what happened to Donna."

Everyone chuckled.

"Thanks so much for making the dinner and setting such a beautiful table," Antonella said. "I'll help you serve."

"No, no, this is your night off, both of you. Just sit down," Alma said. "And please pass me your plates."

"Does anyone want wine?" Lawrence asked.

"Stan, you pour, let the birthday boy relax."

Antonella grimaced at the mention of the birthday boy and shot him a glare.

When all the plates had been served and the wine poured, Alma smiled around the table and said, "*Buon appetito.*" The others chorused her words. Then forks and knives plunged into the oozing, layered lasagna, whose aroma rose so divinely to their nostrils. Total silence followed while everyone tasted and savored their first forkfuls of the rich, delicious dish. Hums of pleasure and gratitude followed.

"*Squisito*, Mamma," Lawrence said.

"*Buonissimo*," Natalie echoed.

"To die for," Stan said with a smile.

Alma beamed, and conversation about food instantly

broke out around the table. But the conviviality was soon interrupted by the doorbell, and Lawrence jumped up to answer it. "Must be Matt and Donna," he said, but returned with only Matteo, who bore a strong resemblance to him, though shorter with softer flesh.

"Sorry I'm late," Matteo said, dropping his motorcycle helmet on the sideboard and sliding into one of the empty chairs. "Hello everyone and happy birthday, bro. Where're the kids?"

"Asleep, and where's Donatella?" Alma said.

"Downstairs, crashing your neighbors' shindig. She spotted an old flame on that ramp and went in to find him. I waited a while, but then gave up."

"How embarrassing," Alma said, passing a plate of lasagna to Matteo. "I hope the Wagners don't mind."

Natalie raised her wine glass. "I'd like to toast the cook and the birthday boy."

"Here, here," the others chimed, raising their glasses.

"And, after dinner, I'd like to do a sketch of you, Lawrence—my contribution to your special day."

"Special indeed," Antonella said with a bite, causing her in-laws to look surprised. "He's been celebrating all day."

At that moment, Augusto the cat leaped onto the sideboard and put his nose to the lasagna.

"Good God!" Alma cried, but before she could get up, Stan had grabbed the cat and dropped him with the thud of four paws to the floor.

"Your lasagna can't be resisted," he said.

"It's the cheese," Alma said.

"Pets can be sly," Natalie said. "Once I was invited to visit the castle on Lake Lugano of my dear friend, Baron von Salis de Merignac. Foolishly, I treated myself to a cashmere coat for the occasion. It was far beyond my budget, but I couldn't resist. When I arrived, the baron hung the coat in his cloakroom. That night, he entertained six of us at one end of the longest table I've ever seen. His adorable terrier joined us for the meal, hoping to catch scraps that accidentally dropped from our forks to his position under the table. The next morning, we were invited to another village for lunch by one of the baron's friends. I went for my coat, and how can I describe the shock I felt when I saw huge holes in it, front and back. I had no idea what had happened. All I could think of was all the money I had spent for the coat and facing my hosts in such a rag."

"God," Matteo laughed. "Was it rats?"

"No, it was the terrier, that little devil. He ate the cashmere as if it were steak."

"Heavens," Alma said.

"Yes, I was weeping inside. But it turned out the baron had insurance that covered the damage. I had to go back to the shop for a receipt to prove the purchase, and wait till you hear what the shopkeeper told me. The same thing had happened to him. He wore cashmere pants to an elegant dinner and kept shaking his legs to shoo off some pest under the table—he suspected a rat, which spoiled his appetite. After the dinner, when he stood up to follow the men to the smoking room, he found the hemline of his trousers had risen three inches. A terrier under the table had eaten his pants."

They all laughed. The story was outlandish, but then

Natalie was always telling such stories, as if her life had been one long chain of disasters.

The doorbell rang again and Donatella joined them. Her svelte body in a miniskirt swept into the room, and she dropped a kiss on the top of Lawrence's head. "Happy birthday, bro. Sorry I'm late, everyone." Her long legs slipped easily into the middle seat between Matteo and Natalie. Alma handed her a plate of lasagna.

"Thanks, Mamma! Looks yummy—your lasagna's the best."

"It's just this, nothing else, except the cake."

"Perfect, you're so good to us. I was just downstairs saying hi to Vico Palombo—remember him? My first crush after my divorce? We couldn't stop chatting—it reminded me how well we got along until we didn't. He may be worth a second try."

"I thought you were serious about Arturo," Alma said.

"I'm 'in love' with Arturo, and as we all know, 'in love' is usually a fleeting, delicious moment that's blind to any unlikable traits in the other person, such as narcissism, which men have a monopoly on. But I love 'in love'—it's about desire, desire ruling us—one of the best feelings in life. So, that's where I'm at with Arturo, and if something more develops—great. I sent him a dozen red roses today."

"You sent roses to a man?" Alma said.

"Why are you surprised?" Stan said.

"It's a good test," Antonella said.

Donatella grinned. "That too, but actually, I sent them in a moment of pure inspiration. When I saw them, I instantly thought of him and felt he'd love getting them from me.

Traditional gender roles never crossed my mind."

"I believe women can have full equality with men," Natalie said, "but, because of men's ultrasensitive egos, women need to cloak their equality in subtle ways, the ways society has conveniently created for them from the beginning of time, when men hunted or tilled and women handled the home."

"Women hunted and tilled too, and they harvested," Antonella said. "They put up the food for winter and cared for the animals, the children, and the family's literacy. They handled illness, births, and death. They wove cloth and sewed clothes. Do you know what it was like to wash bedding and laundry by hand for a family of eight or fifteen?"

"Thank you, Toni, most people just never get it," Donatella said.

"I certainly get it, but I meant we women don't have to *brandish* our superiority," Natalie said.

Everyone laughed, the women in agreement and the men with forbearance.

"I love men," Donatella said, savoring the taste of her lasagna as if savoring men. "But, they're generally less productive than women because of the amount of time they spend focusing on their egos. And the greatest men in history have had wives working full-time for them, not just in the home but as their unacknowledged assistants."

"Alma has always been the business side of our shop," Stan said, "and unacknowledged by the outside world. I like to say that she's got the mind, I've got the hands, and we both have the eye."

"Thank you, Stan," Alma said.

"It's a given men love us because we're capable and willing to self-sacrifice and support their careers. Unfortunately, that paradigm is part of the patriarchal system we need to dismantle, because it includes domestic violence, rape, and being in bondage to men's sex drive, even when they stray. The balance sheet is so unequal that relationships rarely survive."

"Oh, Donatella!" Alma said. "You forget about feelings—men have feelings for us—love, they love us."

"But do you want women to accept being abused or cheated on because of an 'ideal' of love? Come on, Mamma."

Alma sighed. "I want women to be treated fairly, of course."

"Relationships and the patriarchy have been my entire practice," Donatella said. "Couples begin with passion—that can't be helped, that's life, it's wonderful, and for the most part, at that stage it's fairly equal. But then married life settles in, children are born, and mothers naturally—and also inevitably, given the masculine-feminine imbalance—focus on the kids. Sex life wanes, but also for other, natural reasons—boredom, the longing for new stimulation to satisfy the sex drive, fantasies, and, bottom line, the ego."

"On both sides," Antonella said.

"Yes, but fewer women act on it. They're too busy with the kids and being productive for the family, and also getting involved in outside pursuits or careers."

"I respect you, Donna—your career has been a service to others—but do we always have to talk about men, women, and sex at every family meal?" Stan said.

"What else rules our lives, Papa? Be honest."

"Well, what rules my life has changed as I age. How many

couples my age come to you?"

"Fewer, though you'd be surprised. And I agree, the sex drive changes over time—in both sexes—but it never goes away, at least not psychologically." She gave Stan a loving smile. "I really appreciate that you and the men in our family make a sincere effort to support women's equality, even though every now and then your inborn chauvinism pops out."

"And you don't let us get away with it," Stan said.

"How else can we hope to change the patriarchy?"

"Could we please change the subject? This is my birthday," Lawrence said.

Antonella's anger burst out. "Said just like a man! 'Don't make me listen to my weaknesses, let's celebrate my birthday instead, it's been such a wonderful day so far, being a man, being free to do whatever I please, because I'm all that matters!'"

"Ooh," Donatella said. "What happened?"

"Ask him!" Antonella said, standing up and throwing her cloth napkin into Lawrence's face. She strode off, leaving the others in shock.

"Fuck, Larry, what did you do?" Donatella said.

That was the last thing Antonella heard before sealing herself off in the bedroom suite. She sat down on the bed in darkness, the sounds of the party downstairs wafting up to her. The music and lively voices felt unreal, the world felt unreal. She couldn't get a grip on all the feelings and thoughts pounding inside her. It felt even worse that she was now alone while the others remained at the table talking about her. Donatella would be grilling her brother, while the others listened wide-eyed. Antonella hadn't meant to involve them, but her anger had erupted on its own. She dreaded talking to Lawrence and got up to lock the door, but then changed her mind because locking the door would only postpone their confrontation. He would talk to her through the door, she would resist him childishly, and they'd just waste time. But she couldn't imagine what they would say, how they would ever bridge the gap that now existed between them, the total severance she was feeling. She tried to put herself in his shoes, for it was true that her eye also wandered. But she hadn't ever acted on her fantasies—would she if the right person and the right moment came along? Would temptation cast its crazy spell? Would she lose consciousness of her family, of loyalty and trust? She thought it would take a lot for that to happen, partly because of the dramatic change in how men viewed her now that she was married, which didn't happen to married men. Women still noticed married men. This inequality, this double standard in marriage that lowered the value of women, enraged her, even more than Lawrence's stupid lust for a body, which could happen to her as well. And, she felt disgust for his callous use of a young woman who would be forever wounded. It wasn't likely a forty-three-year-old woman could do the same damage to a much younger man. In fact, the woman would still be the victim, stigmatized, ridiculed for her withering age with a young lover—called a cougar. It was horrible!

Antonella took off her dress and hung it in the closet. She got into bed and pulled the covers up to her ears. She shut her eyes, wanting to stop further thoughts, wanting oblivion or sleep. She ached to go back to a time when she lived alone in her cozy turret and woke each morning with total freedom. But then she wouldn't have Rita and Angelo, and the thought of their little faces and high-pitched voices, their laughter and innocence, filled her heart with a flood of love so painful that it felt strangely like solace. Love and grief, their blend the deepest essence of life.

Soon she heard the family and Natalie leaving, for the master bedroom was next to the front door. After murmured good nights, the door closed and silence ensued. She waited, stiff and alert, but Lawrence didn't come to the bedroom. Soon she could hear him cleaning up in the kitchen and imagined he felt too confused and upset to know how to initiate a conversation. She wondered if this was the first calamity in his personal life. She felt relieved he was buying time in the kitchen, for she wasn't ready to talk to him either.

In the kitchen, Lawrence loaded the dishwasher on automatic pilot, his mind trying to make sense of what felt like a shattered world, something beyond his ability to fix. Images of the dinner table, scraps of conversation, made chaos inside his head—Antonella's anger and disgust, how she threw the napkin in his face—and his mother's eyes with disbelieving tears, his father's head sunk in his hands, Donatella's voice saying, "*Stupido!*"

Everything played back.

"Oh, Lorenzo … the children." Alma's lips quivered. "You have to do something, the children are ours too!"

"No, they're not, Mamma," Donatella said. "They belong to Lawrence and Antonella. I know a good couples therapist,

Larry, I think that's your only hope, and you'll be lucky if she agrees. You didn't marry a woman you could push over."

"I didn't push her over."

"Then, what's your definition of respect?"

"Fuck. This sucks," Matteo said, pushing back his chair, taking his helmet from the sideboard, and walking off.

The others got up too.

"I wish you luck, bro, call if you need me," Donatella said, giving Lawrence's shoulder a pat.

Now Lawrence was preparing to face Antonella, who might well refuse to hear him—and he agreed—what good was an apology? He had betrayed their relationship, their love, their trust. He tried to make a plan, rehearse. He could knock on the bedroom door or just carefully open it a crack and ask permission to enter. What if she had locked it? Then he'd have to speak through the wood and be prepared if she yelled back that he should leave, pack a bag and get out—forever! His chest hurt—the area around his heart—it was all tight, constrained, and painful. Somehow, he had to turn this around, but how? Perhaps he should simply ask her what she wanted, after all it was her choice, though he'd do his best to keep them together.

He dried his hands on a dish towel and went to the bedroom door and knocked. Antonella didn't answer, so he slowly opened it. She was under the covers, her back to him, but he knew she was awake. He could feel her tension throbbing in the air. He went to the edge of the bed and looked down at her, but all he could see was the wild foliage of her hair.

"Hey," he said. "I'm sorry. I totally fucked up. And I know it doesn't help to say I'm sorry, but I am. I don't know where my head was. I wasn't thinking, obviously—I mean, how dumb was that? You and the kids are my whole life, all I want, all I've ever wanted. I love you. I love you in a place where there's no definition of love."

"I know, dickhead," she said, her voice hard against the pillow.

Surprise rushed over him. He hadn't expected that answer, and it gave him a jolt of hope.

"It wasn't an affair, it wasn't a relationship. It was ... it was yuck, disgusting office sex."

Her face came up for a moment. "I'd love to have office sex—what a treat!—all those foreign diplomats with exotic accents—but I haven't, I've resisted."

Lawrence stared in surprise. "Well, thanks for being true to me ... I hope you'll believe my heart is true to you, and I'll never forget ... it was crazy, totally wrong."

She didn't answer. He stepped closer to the bed. "Okay if I join you?—easier to talk that way ... in case we talk more."

"Suit yourself," she grumbled. She was mad, but she wasn't throwing him out. He quickly undressed and got into the bed next to her, keeping his body respectfully separate from hers.

But Antonella felt him anyway. She felt his body heat, his male form, his legs with hair, his torso with hair, and his male member resting on his thigh. Everything about him pulsed out in her direction, drawing her like a magnet. Her anger and resentment sizzled like live wires between them as she tried to resist the scent of his skin, which had always been such a turn-on for her. She burned to shake him, pound him, and feel his contrite submission. She forcefully thrust her full length against him. "You bastard! You jerk!"

His breath fell on her like a sigh of relief, as her chastening was just what he wanted, what he needed for his redemption. His hand took her hip as if to defend himself from the rough knocks of her body. But mainly, he gave himself to her attack—the wonder of it—her shifting and striking against him.

"I feel so trapped, so used!" she said, pushing him to his back with sudden feline strength and pinning his shoulders with her knees, throttling his neck with her fingers. "You're so full of yourself! You're gross!"

He clasped her waist, then grabbed her breasts, as if this clutch would stop her strangling him. She fell down on him, her anger releasing fully. "I'm fucking stuck with you!"

Stuck with him—his arms tightened around her—stuck meant staying. But she broke free again, as if rejecting that notion, and rolled off of him. But it was too late and they both knew it, desire was all over them, hot, in flames, like their first years, and their arms and limbs couldn't separate, hers fierce, his receptive. Her body hammered him from the side and she bit his upper arm—that manly muscle. He made an injured noise but loved his angry tigress and swung her around easily, knowing just what she loved—his strength, his hardness in her. But she kept up her battle, and it only fed his excitement to let her win. All he had to do was be there for her, however she wanted him. Finally, she began to melt and sigh, brandishing her last flames of fury as they rolled around, first one on top and then the other. He felt the weakening in her arms and the whimpering of her spirit, and finally, the ultimate surrender to her climax, that divine, convulsive peak that he could feel inside her.

As she came down from those heights and blinding lights, her head collapsed in his armpit. He held on to her, wanting the moment to last forever. Slowly she came to, stirring her head, waking to thoughts and reality. She marveled that she had just dealt with her anger by making love to him. How inexplicable was that? She had been finished with him, trapped by him, and then madly, fiercely fused with him, as if that were the only way they could work out their feelings. Then the thought came to her that she was the second woman he had made love to that day. She writhed in disgust and wrenched off the bed to go shower.

Roma

Antonella sat under a large café umbrella next to the American screenwriter Florian Maye in the Pantheon's ancient piazza. The area had been blocked off to traffic for the afternoon's shooting of a love scene in Florian's crime drama that Gene and Woody were producing. They had become filmmaking partners after their first successful documentary on Albanian immigrants in Italy. The film had explored the Albanians' criminalization by the media for prostitution, drugs, theft, and human trafficking. The narrator's sensitive interviews and the film's historical research revealed the barriers refugees faced when seeking employment, housing, and better futures in Italy, following Albania's political crisis and civil war when communism fell in the 1990s. The film had won festival awards, allowing the new partners—Gene and Woody—to make Gene's transgender thriller, another success.

Florian, the grandson of a Hollywood mogul, had written several moderately successful films and was now financing his latest, *Rattrap*, set in Rome, a city he knew only from a rollicking visit in his early twenties. Antonella had translated the script and then continued to work on the film as Florian's translator. He was on call throughout the day to rewrite scenes and dialogues to fit the actual locations chosen to comply with the city's regulations. He also had to communicate with the director, Dante Di Natale, who didn't speak English.

It was late July, and the sun beat down relentlessly on the square. Not even the fountain's cascading water could give the illusion of refreshment. Florian appeared to be dozing behind his shades and straw hat, a glass of iced tea in front of him. Curious onlookers stood along the barricaded edges of the set to watch the glamorous world of moviemaking, especially because a popular TV star—Rodolfo Gentile—was playing the male lead.

Assistant directors called out for silence when Dante gave the signal for the scene's sixth retake. It was a love scene inside the Pantheon's dark portico of massive columns. The character Carlotta, looking seductive in flowing silk, drifted toward Vincenzo, her fugitive, journalist lover, who had just stepped out from one of the columns' shadows for a stolen tryst. Vincenzo had exposed dealings between the Mafia, the government, the Church, and the media, and now lived under a death sentence while seeking legal protection. Their lovers' fingers touched, their eyes met, their lips slowly came together—a close-up shot. But Dante's voice once again cracked out, "Cut!" The lovers' faces glistened with sticky sweat. Dante cursed Rome's heat and then fell back in his chair as if he had fainted. Bianca Conti, who was playing Carlotta, hurried over to him, followed by Gene, Woody, and Natalie, the last of whom spent many hours on the set, loving the film world's mystique.

Antonella stayed where she was under the umbrella—they didn't need another body hovering over Dante. She had her own way of dealing with Rome's heat, and that was by staying perfectly still in her sheer cotton shift. In stillness, the heat touched her but didn't penetrate her skin. And besides, she was content to stare at Florian's lean body and bone-thin face, the features sharp under taut, tanned skin. His head under the hat was nearly shaved, the gray bristles producing a chic look. And she loved his mouth, the fine shapely lips that invited kissing. They had become lovers quite quickly. It was inevitable that they would notice each other, working so closely on revisions to his script and translating for him all day, but their attraction had ignited immediately, the moment Woody introduced them and they shook hands, with eyes meeting and senses immediately sparking to life with that inner intuition of love's potential. Later, she wondered if it was his air of indifference, his "do as I please" attitude that had allured her, or just his tall, arrogant good looks. Even those thin lips that could sneer so easily fascinated her, for at rest or lost in a reverie, they had the soft tenderness of a woman's or a child's lips. He could be witty, caring, or cynical from one moment to the next and was always tense, unless asleep, as he seemed to be now, with his legs stretched out and his head dropped back, revealing his Adam's apple. In bed, he was a passionate poet, scribbling and reciting effusive lines about her, or reading sonnets by Shakespeare or the Romantics that attested to his feelings. How could she resist such extravagant attention, such a show of adoration? It had been so long since she felt "in love," and she pushed away thoughts of the film wrapping in two more weeks and his return to LA.

Florian was divorced and Antonella was separated from Lawrence. After his fateful forty-third birthday the year before, she had asked for some time alone to soul search what she wanted for her life. Neighbors had rented Lawrence their furnished studio on the top floor of their building. But he was around the house most evenings to be with the kids. There had been a two-week break when Stan and Alma took the children and their Moroccan au pair, Jasmine, to the family's vacation home in Sardinia. Antonella had spent those glorious nights with Florian at his hotel. But now the kids were back and Antonella made sure she came home every night, even if sometimes very late—long after the kids had gone to bed.

She knew Alma strove to save the marriage by keeping the family actively together, food always on the table to share, and the kids assured of quality care. Antonella loved and respected her mother-in-law. She was a gentle, generous, and loving soul, and undoubtedly a surrogate mother to Antonella, the kind of mother she had never had, or not in the way of a true relationship, which came so naturally to the Rowinski-Gasparis. Even when they argued, love and loyalty were a given. Until Florian, Antonella had felt grateful to be part of their clan and had expected that eventually her breach with Lawrence would be repaired. Instead, she had taken refuge in her old, safe independence—nothing could hurt her when she was alone. And now she had fallen in love. She fully embraced the thrilling sensation of "new love," aware of how it wiped out real-world responsibilities. Its euphoria, like a delirium, possessed her and even made her willing to forget about the kids, abandon them. In her love daze, she entertained fantasies of traipsing through an unknown and exciting future with Florian, and no kids were part of it. Awareness of her state alarmed her when she was with the children and forced to face the realities of her current life. She knew she was caught in a restless longing that could bring only short-term fulfillment, and in the long run, disaster. But she couldn't tear herself away. That was the power of "in love."

It was so hot that the piazza's pavement was like the bottom of an oven, its heat rising upward while the sun beat downward. People were trapped inside the scorching oven. The dun-colored buildings seemed to droop in humid fatigue, mirroring the pink impatiens hanging lifelessly from window boxes.

Florian's languid hand reached out in her direction, but the rest of him didn't move. His lofty, nasal voice drawled into the sultry air. "Antonella, please tell Dante we're done with these retakes. It's too fucking hot, and the scene's erotic, not sweaty."

"Looks like he's done, anyway," Antonella said, also glad to be done. Staring at Florian in the heat had aroused her desire for him. She was ready to retreat to his darkened, air-conditioned hotel room, where they could lie on the bed and feel the cool air tingling over their skin until they turned to each other to fulfill their sensual craving. He was on the same wavelength, and with head still tipped but turned toward her, he said, "Come here, gorgeous, taste me."

"I have been," she said, sliding out of her chair and leaning over his head to kiss his lips, a light dab at first, then a touch with the tip of her tongue on his teeth, then meeting his own tongue as if tongues were curious entities in their own right. Finally their mouths sealed with passion, passion that sent sensations coursing through her body with a wonderful urgency. His arms pulled her down into his lap, with a bit of clanging from the metal table and chair that she bumped coming down.

"Let's get out of here," he said.

"Okay, you two, break it up. Where do you think you are? Rome?" Gene said.

Natalie and Woody were with him, and they stepped under the umbrella's shade. Woody wore a blue shirt, white linen pants, a Panama hat, and shades—the dapper producer. Gene was shaggy and biting as always.

Antonella stood up.

"We're done for today," Gene said. "It's 103. Tomorrow's going to be the same."

"In that case, I'm rewriting this scene for the Alps, and we can get out of Rome as soon as possible. Come on, Toni, we can rewrite this scene in my nice-and-cool hotel."

"We're going to shoot this scene early tomorrow. We extended the permit. Crew's coming at five, actors start at seven," Woody said. "The portico will be dark and romantic."

"So let's all go for a swim," Gene said. "The van's waiting."

"Lovely!" Natalie said. "Which pool? Antonella's club?"

"No," Woody said, "too much Cassia traffic, and it's a family place with kids peeing in the pool. Let's go to my golf club, it has a great pool, and a bar."

"Perfect," Gene said.

"Let's invite Dante, it'll improve his mood," Natalie said.

Everyone knew Natalie had a crush on the sixty-year-old director and liked chatting with him. "He's occupied," Gene said. "Didn't you hear him accept Bianca's offer for a massage?"

"Oh … then what's happened with Rodolfo? I thought—"

"The director's got more clout for her career. Come on folks, your limo's waiting." He waved toward his white van parked on the edge of the piazza.

"Nah, you all have fun," Florian said, putting a possessive arm around Antonella. "We're going to work on the script."

"In Italy we do things in groups," Gene said. "We're one big happy family."

"Then Italy can learn from America that twosomes are more fun."

"Nope, I've lived in both countries, and groups win, hands down. Did Antonella ever tell you about our—"

"Now, Gene," Natalie interrupted, "you're an incorrigible provocateur. You haven't changed one iota since the first day I met you, which only proves men don't evolve."

"Nor has that refrain of yours," Gene retorted.

"No kidding," Woody laughed. "I've heard it for fifty years."

Natalie slid her arm affectionately through Woody's and smiled up at him. "Fifty years of true and lasting friendship."

"And most of them divorced," Woody said, patting her hand.

"I have a lifetime of memories. And from our separate apartments, and mostly our separate countries, you've always known my minutest thought, like telepathy." She turned to the others. "It's taken us almost to the grave to realize, we've actually been husband and wife all these years, and that no one else will ever come close to reaching us on that divine level. It's like being in the womb together."

"I wouldn't go that far," Woody laughed.

"Congratulations, you've found the ideal *arrangement*," Florian said with the French pronunciation. "Never any husband-wife spats, never any claustrophobia, just freedom and a best friend. You should write a how-to book for the rest of us—you'd make millions."

"I don't need to," Woody said, flashing a grin.

"And we have news, since one hour ago," Natalie said, squeezing Woody's arm.

"That's right, the love scene—however miserable in this heat—brought it on. Another good reason to get to my club for some chilled Prosecco," Woody said.

"What news?" A big smile spread over Antonella's face. "Like … wedding bells?"

"You tell them, Woody. Then I'll know it's real."

"Fine. It's like this—now that Natalie and I have reached the twilight years of our lives, we've decided to marry again and live together, but keep her apartment for when we're mad at each other."

"He's agreed to eat dinner after eight and not harangue me about how I spend money or waste time at cafés with my friends."

"And she's agreed not to flirt in front of me."

"That's going to be hard, because we have different interpretations of flirting."

"Not true. You were born a flirt. Back in the day, you were the hottest ticket on via Veneto, a terrible tease, and you loved it, you sought it."

Natalie warmed at this description of herself. She gave him another squeeze. "Thank you, darling."

"You were never satisfied till you knew every man in your orbit was madly in love with you."

"No, no, I never led men on like that. I was always just myself, true to myself."

Florian was searching Natalie's octogenarian face for traces of her past allure. "Were you really like that?"

"My dear young man, I was no different from your young lady here." Her eyes swept over Antonella.

"I'm not like that," Antonella said.

"That's right," Woody said, "Antonella doesn't flirt."

"It depends who you're talking to," Florian said. "Which reminds me, we're splitting. Ta-ta."

"But the van's waiting," Gene said.

"Flor, let's go for a swim with them. It's early, it's hot. Wait till you see Woody's club—it's a spa," Antonella said with a coaxing smile.

"Damn," he said. "Do I really have to do this Italian group thing?"

"I think you do," Gene said.

Woody's club felt like a tropical paradise, with its lazy palms and tilted umbrella pines rising high in the sapphire sky, while a fiery sun blazed down on a luscious pool and an undulating, verdant golf course. People were quite content in the heat because of the water, not only the rippling pool, but also the giant showerheads next to it. People who didn't want to go into the pool—like Natalie—could stand under these pleasant rainfalls.

Antonella reclined on a lounge chair in the red bikini she always kept in her satchel during the summer. She was enjoying watching the scene while Florian dozed on his stomach on the chaise next to her, wearing borrowed shorts from Gene. His left arm hung down to the pavement and he seemed asleep. An umbrella pine shaded them. Antonella could hear Gene schmoozing with a prospective investor, the two of them waist-deep in the shallow end of the pool. "Our first film won a Donatello, which leveraged us, but we're lucky with the current one because an American is financing it—he's the guy over there snoozing. And the beauty in the red bikini is his full-time interpreter—if you get what I mean. Anyhow, stop by the office—we're always looking for investors for our next projects. We've got a few in development."

Antonella smiled. Gene always hard at work, and the partnership with Woody had allowed him to fulfill his dreams. Now she heard Natalie chatting away with an older, overweight man in the shower next to her. He wore a men's bikini that his rolls of fat nearly hid. Natalie wore a turquoise swimsuit that flattered her petite lines. Woody sat under an umbrella, reading the newspaper. Everyone was relaxed.

Florian's hand groped blindly for Antonella and landed on her breast. He gave it a squeeze with a pleasurable groan, then let his hand slide down to rest on her damp belly. "This group thing's going to kill me," he said.

"We can go. We've cooled off."

"Good, I'm ready to devour you." His chaise creaked as he got up.

Antonella also rose and reached for her dress. "And then I have to head home," she said with a rueful smile.

"Don't remind me."

He watched her pull her dress over her head with a wistful expression. She wondered if he was thinking the same thing as she—that ultimately their affair was doomed because of her kids. Florian looked down and stepped into his flip-flops. He draped his shirt over the top of his satchel.

"We're heading out," Antonella called out to the others.

"What? So soon? It isn't even six. Aren't you coming to dinner with us?" Natalie said from her shower.

"Don't be naive," Woody said, and then smiled at them. "Have fun, kids, see you tomorrow. Come before seven."

"I really don't see myself as a kid," Florian said. "I'm almost fucking fifty."

"Well, when you're eighty-three, it's all relative," Woody said.

"What I want to know, amigo, is, when you're eighty-three, do you still have to put up with having one thing on your mind most of the time?"

"Depends who you ask. But if you want my opinion, yes. You just can't do it that easily anymore, and you don't crave it as much, maybe because of the faulty equipment. It's easier for women, they have no problem in that department. But mainly, what I marvel at, is seeing young lovers—I mean the really young ones—and not being able to remember myself at that hormonally raging time—those feelings, that passion, that drive—that virile male body."

"Shh!" Natalie said. "This isn't pool talk, darling." Then she laughed at the fat man next to her and told him in a mix of English and Italian, "My fiancé is such a philosopher. And can you believe?—we've been divorced most of our lives, but now we're getting married again, in two weeks, right here, at this club." She wagged her hips playfully. "It's such a lark, *dottore*, and you're invited too!"

Her *dottore* responded in a fusillade of Italian.

"What the hell was that?" Florian said.

"High-speed Italian," Antonella said.

"Does Lawrence know about your boyfriend?" Gene said, joining them, his swimsuit dripping and forming a puddle at his feet.

"Who's Lawrence?" Florian said.

"My husband, remember?"

"Oh yeah—the reason I forgot. Come on, babe, let's blow this joint. Not that I didn't like being here. I'm glad we came. Thanks everyone, thanks Woody—nice setup you have."

"You'll be back, I hope—the wedding party, the day after we wrap."

"I wouldn't miss it. I'm learning to survive the Italian-group thing."

"I must say, I'm going to miss you when you go back to the States," Woody said. "You spike things up."

"No, he's a bit too rude," Natalie said, but with a smile.

She pointed her toe in the shower's spray. "Although, maybe it's his antagonistic streak that fascinates. It's like a current, an undertow—it drags you against your will into his sphere."

They all laughed.

"Thank you, Natalie, I rather like that depiction of myself, even though Toni knows another side of me, one you'll never see—the Keats, Byron, Shelley side."

"I don't doubt that, Mr. Suave, but why rush off? It's only six o'clock." She gave him a dazzling smile from her glistening face. "This is Roma. You're missing out on our magic if you go back to your hotel room and hole up for the rest of the night. So much more remains."

"Better than Toni?"

"You'll still have Toni at the end of the night, and all the better for waiting while being tempted for so long."

"Natalie loves the streets," Woody said.

"I love Rome. And at this hour, we socialize with coffee or a drink and stroll the beautiful streets, admiring the elegant windows full of handcrafted art. We find the perfect trattoria for dinner, where we relax over food and conversation—connection, Florian, connection."

"I'm not tempted."

"We stroll again after dinner to aid our digestion, we even stop at a bar for a *digestivo*. By then, Rome has cooled. Rome has become dark, and in Rome's darkness, something indescribable happens to the human psyche—something like an altered state, one of inner exhilaration—of flight—and we embody it, like an aphrodisiac, like a potent drug. That's when it's time to say good night and head off alone with our lovers."

"I like that. There's still time to work it into my script," Florian said.

"Good, but you need to experience it to write it."

"Exactly," Gene said, "I vote we go to Tivoli for dinner and eat under the empire's stars."

"There's always a nice breeze up there," Antonella said.

"What?" Florian glared at her. "Whose side are you on?"

"I can get us there in thirty-five minutes," Gene said, pleased to have needled Florian.

"No, the answer is no, and it's the same word in Italian: no," Florian said. "Antonella and I are leaving. Au revoir, adieu, ciao, bye-bye."

"I've never seen an ego quite like yours," Natalie said.

"He's best when he doesn't talk," Antonella joked.

"Toni, what are you saying?"

"She's saying you have some rough edges," Natalie said with a smile.

Florian dropped his satchel and stepped into the shower between Natalie and her *dottore*. Smiling in a debonair way, he put his right arm around her waist, lifted her right hand with his left, and began dancing gracefully with her while the shower sprinkled them. He hummed and then sang, "Do you wanna dance, and hold my hand, tell me I'm your lover man…"

Everyone tittered. Natalie looked so tiny next to Florian's spare height. They moved in a gentle, sensual circle. Natalie's initial surprise gave way to playing along with the part Florian had contrived. She tossed back her head with a gay laugh and said, "You silly young man! I couldn't have guessed you knew how to dance."

Florian swept her into a turn under his arm, and she bumped into the *dottore*, whose bulk had strayed over the line into their shower. "Bug off, fatso," Florian said airily, and then to Natalie, "he doesn't speak English, right?"

"Certainly not enough to know *that* English," Natalie said tartly.

"I want you to know, Natalie, that your future husband is a very lucky man," Florian said, as he slowed their dance to a standstill and gave a little bow.

"And you are a very naughty boy, but fun. It's your undertow." She laughed and shook a finger at him. "But be forewarned, women know you're not a safe bet for the long haul."

Florian's lips gave their sardonic twist, and to finish off the scene, he bent down and kissed her on the lips, lingering there a little too long and confusing her, as well as everyone else.

Antonella took his elbow and pulled him out of the shower. "Come on, Florian, this isn't a movie."

"I know, but I'm a writer, and I have to test every possible scenario," he said, and then, with a facetious gleam in his eye for Antonella, he added for the others' benefit, in his devious way, "I adored the way you took command of me just then, my love. It's something we must explore—as soon as we're finally alone."

Woody laughed. "You're a great actor, Florian, we have to create a part for you before the film ends."

"I can come up with something just right for him." Gene laughed.

"Screw you," Florian said. "Ta-ta, my friends. *A domani.* And fuck everything."

The house was still busy when Antonella got home that night. Alma, Stan, and Jasmine were in the kitchen cleaning up after a late dinner—perhaps they had waited for her. Antonella could hear Lawrence singing with the kids in their bedroom. She poked her head into the kitchen to say a quick hello and thank-you. But Alma was eager for more conversation and followed Antonella into the narrow hallway that led to the rest of the apartment. "Such long hours, Toni! Did you eat?"

"Yes, always plenty of food on the set." She heard herself lie and felt awful. She had been goofing off with her lover, while others worked for her children and her own personal freedom.

Alma's warm brown eyes, so much like Lawrence's, searched her face. "Does that writer really need you this late?"

"He's pretty dependent, but luckily we wrap in two weeks," she said, stepping away, more to escape her feelings of being a guilty adolescent again than to escape Alma, the worried parent. She glanced back and tried to smile, but it was more like an apology for being a bad person.

"I hope when he leaves you'll come back to us … the little ones need you, Lawrence too. We all need you."

Antonella nodded and made her escape to the kids' room. She felt consumed by guilt. Here was home, Lawrence putting the kids to bed the way she also loved putting them to bed, except in her current, in-love state, she didn't even want to be there. This scene—her home—felt unreal, disconnected from her, and yet she knew it was the most connected thing to her in her life. She just couldn't feel it, not now, not while dwelling in a magical realm with Florian, a realm that existed only in her senses and fantasies. Here, right in front of her, was reality—family and growing children, true and lasting love. Why couldn't she feel it? Why did her affair with Florian blot out everything except the thrill of their attraction? He was leaving in two weeks. That would force decisions. If she promised to join him later, would she really do it?

In the children's room, Lawrence sat on the floor between the twin beds, leaning against the night table. The kids' English and Italian books were scattered by his legs, and he stopped singing when Antonella came in. The kids let out a whoop and popped out of their covers to receive hugs and kisses from Antonella.

"Nonna took us swimming today," Rita said. "I can jump in now. I want you to see me!"

"I can't wait to see you! We'll go to the pool this weekend," she answered.

The twins chortled and wiggled back down under their covers.

"*Buona notte, tesori,*" Lawrence said, kissing and ruffling their silken heads while they giggled. Then he moved away for Antonella's turn, switching off the light as he left. He waited for her in the front hall.

"Can we talk for a minute—outside?" he said when she joined him.

Dread filled her, but she made her voice sound normal.

"I'm so tired—it was so hot today, a really brutal day."

"But we need to talk, or I do."

"After the film—it ends in two weeks."

"No, I'm not waiting two weeks to talk about us. I've waited more than a year. "

"Not now, Larry, I'm sorry."

His lips pressed grimly. "I guess you're having an affair with that writer on the film, and that's why you don't want to talk."

Fear seized her. Hearing him say the truth felt like being caught red-handed. She had no desire to confess. But before she could find a way to put him off, buy more time, her cell phone rang. She reached into her satchel, grabbed it, and clicked it off, assuming it was Florian, full of love messages in the aftermath of their time in bed together. He often called her at night to purr streams of poetic-consciousness into her ear.

Lawrence also assumed it was her lover, so that when the phone rang again, he grabbed it from her and answered it with a high "Mmm?" that passed for a feminine tone. Florian burst into his recitations, while Lawrence listened and dodged Antonella's lunges.

"My God, Antonella, you were wonderful tonight! The bed's still warm with your love, your fragrance. I can't stop thinking about you! I've already penned a dozen poems and want to read them while you lie there in the dark!"

"Give me that!"

Lawrence flipped the top over the phone, eyes blazing. "*Cazzo!*" he swore.

"Well, you got what you wanted!" she shouted.

"This is *my* home, *my* family, and no idiotic *americano* is going to disrupt that."

At that moment, the elder Rowinski-Gasparis tiptoed through the hallway, murmuring good night with sympathetic looks as they passed through the front door. The interruption calmed Lawrence just enough to hand Antonella her phone, when he had intended to throw it across the room. "I'm gonna kill that prick! I was never serious, I was just stupid. Why are you paying me back?"

"I'm not paying you back! For God's sake, we aren't living together, we're separated. And I'm too exhausted for this conversation! Please go, please leave me alone!"

"No! This can't wait. I just heard that douchebag—he's crazy about you. And my kids are not moving to LA!"

She pressed her hands to her head, which was swimming. "Please, Larry." She went to the door and opened it. "Please go!"

He glared at her. "I'm not a dog going upstairs to his doghouse every night. This is my home, my family, and I want to come back. I want to live here, with you. It's been over a year, and it's time to heal what happened."

"I hear you, and we'll talk, but after the film." She left him and went to the bedroom suite and closed the door. She cried. Everything shattered inside, beyond her ability to resolve. She had no idea what she should do. All she could feel was destruction, the force of destruction moving in.

Lawrence left the apartment, his mind racing to find a solution. He understood that it was impossible to reach Antonella the way she was—"in love"—which infuriated him, but it was up to him to do something to bring their lives back together. If she wouldn't listen, wouldn't talk, he would try writing a letter.

The early morning was cool and fresh. Rome always managed to sweep away its previous day's debris. And the morning smelled like Rome — all the ancient stone and millennia of human existence tingled in the new day's soft Mediterranean breeze. Birds chirped as if they inhabited a natural preserve instead of stone, grime, and a pea-green river.

Many Romans had left town for the summer to escape the infamous heat, but the biggest exodus was yet to come with the Ferragosto holiday that launched Italy's month-long hiatus from work. The film was under pressure to wrap before that mass flight to family escapes by the sea, the countryside, or the mountains.

The streets were peaceful when Antonella drove to *centro*. Summer traffic was down, and she could enjoy the graceful curves of the Lungotevere, shaded by overhanging plane trees. The river's marble-faced bridges were empty and as still as the turbid water they crossed. The city's beauty in its quiet mode filled her with inspiration. She didn't think, she only gazed and let Rome's presence permeate her, like one of Rosini's potions that erased physical and mental disturbances.

She parked in one of her secret places near the Pantheon and walked to the set, her legs feeling alive with the morning's energy—not to mention the extra boost of Florian in her bloodstream. She reached the vans lined up along the edge of the piazza. The cameras and grips were ready, and the actors had arrived. She saw Gene and Woody in the middle of all the activity and waved good morning.

Natalie was seated at their usual café, on the other side of the fountain. It faced the ancient monument and the love scene they were sure to finish in the morning's cool currents. Natalie looked elegant, as if she had just stepped out of the makeup artist's trailer—hair sculpted in place, pastel-lemon dress without a wrinkle, and face like a Fabergé egg, royal, exquisite. Antonella smiled—for all the older woman's railing against class and power, she still desired to be seen and known as the Polish countess of her birthright. But in her life, she had made better friends with Americans than with Europeans, perhaps because America represented freedom. Of course, Americans had committed genocide against the indigenous peoples of the New World and had cruelly enslaved Africans for centuries. Now, in the fledgling twenty-first century, America suffered the same gross social divisions and pernicious inequalities of older Western societies, but even so, the idea of America as a free place with equal opportunity somehow prevailed.

Antonella kissed Natalie and sat down.

"I'm dying to tell you, and only you, because we've always shared being women, despite some of our differences."

Antonella smiled and nodded. Before Natalie could delve in, the waiter delivered two espressos. "I ordered for us as soon as I saw you arrive," Natalie said. She poured sugar into her cup and stirred until the dark liquid was like a syrup.

"So, what's on your mind?" Antonella asked.

Natalie took a sip of her coffee. "I want to share that I feel guilty for marrying Woody, or that I'm doing it because I'm so afraid."

"You mean afraid of money?"

"Yes, afraid of destitution. I'm exhausted worrying about it. And it's killing me that I'm doing exactly what I've always detested in others."

"What do you mean?"

"Being a golddigger."

"But you aren't. You're just…" Antonella's voice trailed off.

"Just what?"

"Doing what women always do—feeling guilty. We're conditioned to feel guilty for anything we do, including things that make us feel happy. We're raised to believe we don't deserve to be happy—we're bad no matter what."

They laughed. "It's true," Natalie said. "But still, I didn't say yes to Woody until I felt desperate. That neighbor of mine who promised to buy my apartment all these years is now in jail for money laundering. And Woody, bless him, looked over my taxes and discovered my accountant has been stealing from me. People take advantage of old women, or women period. And young people—even the ones on this film—treat me with forced patience, like I'm not even a person anymore. That's why I said yes to Woody."

"But there are so many other reasons for why you said yes—like love. You and Woody have a lifelong, true-love relationship. It's symbiotic, it's got that cosmic connection that rarely happens."

"Thank you, I believe that. And you have the same kind of relationship with Lawrence. Wait—don't interrupt me. When I saw you arrive just now, I was struck by how pretty you look—like a woman in love. But I know Florian's type and—"

"Shh! Don't spoil my happiness! Lawrence is already doing that."

"Good!"

"Don't be on his side!"

"Believe me, *tesoro*, I understand. I've been there, and it's hard, it's torture to let go of something that feels so good but ultimately it's just desire." She paused with a sympathetic look at Antonella. "Listen, I've never told you this before, but I had an affair when I was married, even though you heard me tell Woody I never cheated."

"I'm not surprised. It's so thrilling to be with someone new."

"Yes, but desire's like any other addiction—we humans keep chasing after it, hoping to make it a permanent state. But that can't happen. And your true love with Lawrence is what's most precious. When passion fades, you still have that uncanny connection—you called it a cosmic connection, and that's what it is. And you'll always have your own life warmed by its love."

"Nicely put, Natalie, and I agree, but for now, I'm going to stay in the love bubble, so no more lecturing."

"I'm done. And just in time—here comes your paramour."

"There she is! Queen of my dreams!" Florian called out as he came across the piazza to their table. He looked fresh in his casual summer clothes, clothes from the shops of Rome. He leaned down to kiss both of them and then sank into the extra chair next to Natalie. "I hope I'm not interrupting your female tête-à-tête?"

"No, I'm glad you're here," Antonella said. "And sorry for

last night."

"Yeah, I finally got to meet the asshole, and cripes I couldn't sleep a wink after that—you going from my arms to his."

"He doesn't live with me. And that's pretty crass."

"Sorry."

"What happened?" Natalie interrupted, eyes wide.

"I'm actually glad he heard me and knows where the two of us stand, or where he stands," Florian said, as he slid folded papers across the table to Antonella. "Here, my love, these are what I wanted to read to you last night."

She took the papers and put them in her satchel with a murmured thanks. She guessed they were his latest love poems, and she loved the attention and flattery.

Florian leaned back on two legs of his chair and folded his arms over his chest—his common pose. "I don't mind at all that you have kids. I want to meet them while I'm still here. My house is big enough for all of us, and it has a pool—kids love pools. I also accept that Italian law makes you wait a few years before you can divorce, I'm okay with that—all I care about is seeing you every day."

"You mean LA over Rome?" Natalie said incredulously. She didn't add—*you* over Lawrence?

"Yeah, LA beats Rome hands down," Florian said with a smug pucker of his lips.

The waiter came by, and he ordered an extra strong *caffè americano*. Then he grinned at Antonella. "I hope you heard me order that all by myself."

"Yes, *bravo, tesoro.*"

He turned to Natalie. "Remind me, when's your wedding reception? Do I need to change my flight?—that is, if I'm still invited."

"Of course you're still invited—after that kiss yesterday, I must have you there," she teased.

"Oh, you liked that, did you? I have to admit it turned out more interesting than I expected."

"You're a lizard, Florian, and no woman is ever going to take you seriously."

"Is that so? Then perhaps you can train me in the secrets of success."

"They don't exist in LA."

Antonella cut in. "It's going to be ten degrees cooler today."

"Good—Rome's fucking killing me."

"I don't understand why you wrote a film set in Rome, when you don't particularly like it," Natalie said.

"I wrote it, Natalie, because love stories set in Rome with a Mafia subplot are box office hits. But I do like Rome, or maybe you're right—maybe I like it mentally more than actually. Or maybe it's just the name I like—Rome."

"I guarantee that as soon as you're back in LA, you're going to miss *Rome*."

"Nope, the only thing I'm going to miss is the most beautiful lady who lives there," he said, smiling with pure tenderness at Antonella. "Which is why I'm taking her home with me."

Antonella laughed. "We haven't talked about that, and I don't want to talk about it now."

Florian finished his coffee and banged down the cup. He flashed a Cheshire Cat grin at the women. "I'm going to fucking miss *caffè americano—lungo, doppio, e eck-stra.*" He pronounced "extra" like the Italians, which meant pulling back his mouth in a grimace to execute the "eck." His chair scraped the cobblestones as he got up, and without looking back, he headed down the slight incline to the set, his body language ruffled.

Those last two weeks of the film, Antonella and Florian continued to live in their lovers' bubble. Antonella managed to avoid further conversation with Lawrence, even though their paths crossed in the apartment. Both kept a polite distance. He had left her a letter soon after their confrontation in the hall the night he had grabbed the phone and listened to Florian's rapturous professions of love. But she had barely read it. Instead, her eyes skimmed over his caring, sincere words with her heart barricaded against them. After that, it was as if a timer had turned on, a timer for the remaining days of the film and being with Florian. And even though Lawrence left her alone, she knew he was fully focused on the situation, and it made her uneasy, as if his presence were lurking and in a canny way would step into her path at the critical moment and make things go his way. It was a side of him she knew from their dating days, when she sensed his mind at work, his intention of getting Gene out of the way to achieve his goal of marrying her. Maybe it was like the footwork strategies he had learned playing soccer.

As the film moved to different locations in Rome during its last days, Florian and Antonella disappeared for long spells from the set, and several times for the entire day. They had their cell phones and could be reached if needed. But no one bothered them—Rome was sympathetic to lovers. And whenever the script needed a rewrite, Gene was there to handle it, and at this point, Florian couldn't care less.

Antonella and Florian wandered everywhere in their love daze. They drove outside the city walls to ancient sites as timeless as their own existence felt. They sat with heads together in restaurants and sealed themselves up in Florian's air-conditioned hotel room. He talked as if their future were already awaiting their arrival in LA, and Antonella let him talk without answering. When he was gone, there'd be time to reflect and decide her future.

The film's last scene took place at the Fontana dell'Acqua Paola, nicknamed the Fontanone, on the Gianicolo hill, overlooking all of Rome. It was a monumental baroque structure that gushed waterfalls into a luscious semicircular basin as blue as the Mediterranean sky above it. Like a glorious oasis on a high plateau, the rushing, rippling water flickered with sunlight that elevated the human spirit, connected it to the infinite beyond.

In this last scene, Vincenzo, cornered by Mafia assassins, was to leap from the monument's summit into the fountain. It was reminiscent of Puccini's *Tosca*, but a modern-day version involving the same kinds of corrupt characters and betrayal in love. Florian hadn't understood the city when he wrote the script, and throughout the shoot, Gene had helped with closer interpretations, as well as better locations, including the Fontanone for the last scene. Now everyone was present and somewhat breathless for Vincenzo's fatal leap. The stunt double was up there with one of the cameras while specialized crew checked the fastenings of the black net stretched over the fountain. With a megaphone, Dante was shouting directions up and down the thundering waterfalls. Florian, Gene, and Woody were at his side, while Antonella watched from the piazza's bordering balustrade.

Suddenly her phone rang. It was her mother calling from California. Bad timing, despite being good to hear from Jenny. Lately she called more frequently and asked more questions about the children and Antonella's life. "Mamma, it's so good to hear from you, but we're in the middle of shooting the film's last scene and I'll have to call you back," Antonella said.

"No problem, sweetie, I just wanted to give you a heads up that Steve and I are coming to Rome next month. He has a conference. Could we stay with you?"

"Of course! We'd love that. The kids have grown so much— wait till you see!"

"I can't wait. And I have so much to tell you. Everything has been coming together for me—all this work of four years—dreams and ancestral healing. It's been totally transformative. I want to tell you about my family's 'disconnect,' and how Papa's family was the same. No one's to blame—that's just the way it is in most families. Trauma and wounds get passed down. Do you know what I mean?"

"You sound so happy, Mamma, I'm so glad!"

"Me too, and for more reasons than my healing work. There's Steve—he's great—we're together now, you probably guessed."

"Yeah, I figured, and I'm happy for you. Does Papa know? Are you going to see him when you come?"

"Yes, I have some things to pick up there. You know he has a girlfriend."

"No, he must hide it when we visit."

"I'm glad he has someone. We have so much to talk about."

"We do, so send your dates, and I'll call you back in a day or so, as soon as everything settles down here."

After their warm goodbyes, Antonella turned her attention back to the fountain, where the cameras, actor, and net were quivering in readiness. It seemed everyone was waiting for her to get off the phone. Dante's voice roared out against the downward thunder of waters, "Action!"

Vincenzo, with a ravaged face, having just learned in the scene before about Carlotta's betrayal in exchange for financial security with one of the mobsters, took his last look at the world—the Eternal City—and then his double flung himself from the fountain's precipice. Quite a bit later, the net removed, they filmed a dummy floating on the fountain's sun-flickering water, with the gushing source of life continuing to splash down, as if nothing had happened a moment before on that golden day. Such was the value of a human life—negligible. Florian was sprawled in a lounge chair next to Dante, basking in his drama's marvelous finale, even though Gene had written it.

That night, everyone partied at a downtown restaurant, and afterward Antonella spent the night with Florian at his hotel. Their mood was soft and bittersweet. They kept saying between kisses, "We'll see each other soon," but the words felt more like wishful thinking than reality for both of them.

The next day—the day of Natalie and Woody's wedding—

they were subdued, looking at each other with sad smiles and eyes. They spent the morning walking Rome's maze of narrow streets—their farewell to the city of their love. Florian didn't even try to promise comparable scenes in LA. They just walked, holding onto each other, and stopping every now and then at a tucked-away bar for another caffè.

In the early evening, after dressing for the wedding party, Antonella joined Florian in front of the large mirror hanging over his hotel bureau. Her eyes admired him—tall, slender, artsy—someone important. He wore a dark blue, no-tuck, embroidered shirt and gray pants. "You look elegant," she said, wrapping an arm lightly around his back so as not to wrinkle his fine linen.

"And you remind me of a cloud—a fatally hypnotizing cloud," he said, turning into her with a smile, and circling her waist with his hands.

She smiled back, for she felt like a cloud in the swishing peach chiffon of her dress.

"You know how I hate these mindless fêtes," he said, "but going with you makes it feel tantalizing."

"You're going to have fun. This is Rome. You'll meet all kinds of characters, right out of a Fellini movie—material for your next script."

"I've got all the material I need right here."

He kissed her, but as his head drew back, he moaned with a catch in his throat, "I don't want you to leave me."

She hugged him, her face lightly pressed to his chest, so she could avoid answering. She marveled at how human beings longed for another person at their side to ease the psychic pain of being alone in life. But at the same time, they pined for freedom, for the flight of a bird, for no ties to anyone or anything. It was such a paradox.

"Everything'll work out," she said softly, consolingly, looking up into his chiseled face. She knew that in a day or two he'd be fine, because nothing in his life was going to change, and that was how he really wanted it, even if he didn't acknowledge it to himself.

They arrived at the club as the sun was setting over the golf course in a fiery orange that not only bid farewell to the day, but also to summer, for the shadows had already changed to the first subtle signs of autumn.

The lawn by the clubhouse had been set up for the party with a band's platform at one end and tables and chairs around the dance area's periphery. A beautiful evening was setting in, and the caterer's staff worked the bar and the buffet tables that bordered the event. Hors d'oeuvres were sizzling on grills and would be followed in an hour or so by a multicourse dinner. The pool was a short distance away, lit by tall spotlights.

Natalie greeted Antonella and Florian as soon as they came through the sliding doors of the clubhouse to the deck that faced the grounds. They kissed and Natalie held out her hand to show her wedding ring. "Can you believe? I saved this. I must have known."

"You made the right choice twice," Florian said, giving her shoulders a squeeze. "I'm going to grab us a table," he told Antonella and headed down the deck steps to the lawn.

"You look beautiful, radiant," Antonella said, giving Natalie another hug.

"Thank you, my dear friend, that's exactly how I feel inside, and I'm glad to know it's showing. I can't wait to see Bianca and find out what's going on. I heard she and Rodolfo are going to Crete tomorrow."

"Oh? What about Dante?"

"Apparently, he got drunk at the party last night and spent the night with the makeup artist, though he swears he thought he was in Bianca's room."

"Better keep an eye on your husband. This is movie business…"

Natalie laughed, her gay, tinkling laugh. "Indeed. He's so appealing, and I never really noticed it the first time around. I was too focused on myself and my own effect. I wasn't prepared for marriage, the commitment. But now I am."

"That means you're prepared to make sacrifices, or you think you are."

Natalie laughed. "I've warned myself to keep my mouth shut when we clash. I hope I can. I'm hot-headed, and I never wanted to admit that. I really hope you'll go back to Lawrence once your wicked boyfriend leaves."

"I'm not going to think about that now."

Natalie suddenly looked guilty. "You know, I have something to tell you."

"What?"

"He called me the other day to congratulate me, and it just popped out—the way it's been popping out to everyone I run into."

"What—are you saying you invited Lawrence?"

She nodded. "But I doubt he'll come. And even if he

did, Toni, there're going to be so many people here, you'd never cross paths."

"Why did you do that? This is my last night with Florian. You've ruined it. I can't believe it! Or maybe I can!"

"I didn't mean to invite him."

"Yes you did. You want us back together, so you meddled. You weren't a loyal friend to me. I'm really upset, Natalie. I need a few minutes alone."

She went down the steps and joined Florian at his table. She said nothing to him about Lawrence being invited, but the party became a tense affair for her, always watching the glass doors on the deck for Lawrence to enter the garden. She was angry, fuming inside at Natalie, and at the same time filled with dread for the moment when Lawrence and Florian would come face to face. She knew Lawrence was coming for that exact purpose. And she would be the person in the middle. It was going to be awful.

An hour went by, while more than a hundred guests wandered the twilight scene, nibbling hot and tasty appetizers, drinking the good wines being poured at the bar, and socializing with happy chatter and affection. Woody and Gene stopped by the table to chat for a while, and others from the film also came by to pay last respects to Florian before his early morning departure. Recorded music had been playing from speakers, but now the band was on the low stage checking their amps for sound before starting to play live music for the long dinner that would be accompanied by dancing.

The guests were eager to eat—the aromas permeating the garden were mouthwatering. The menu included several pasta dishes, followed by grilled meats and seafood. The party was casual, no formal etiquette. Guests were free to get food from the buffet or wait for servers to deliver the courses to their tables. It made for a little bedlam but one that everyone seemed to enjoy—less formality. It was then, as the meal began, that Lawrence arrived with Donatella. They came through the deck's glass doors, and Antonella watched as Lawrence scanned the scene from his higher position, probably looking for her. Donatella looked like a model, tall and skinny in her tight, black minidress. Her dark hair swung freely against her bare shoulders, and strands of colorful beads swayed as she came down the short flight of steps to the party, Lawrence close behind.

Antonella's suspense became more acute. She could take no interest in her food and felt no connection to the party or people stopping to talk to her. Instead, thoughts circled futilely in her head: Why is my last day with Florian being ruined by Natalie and Lawrence? Why am I feeling ashamed to have my lover checked out, as if he weren't good enough? What is Lawrence going to do? I'm afraid of Lawrence. He's here because of me. I think Florian and I should leave right now, avoid what's coming.

But she continued to sit at the table as waiters came and went, removing and delivering plates, and dropping off bottles of red and white wine and water. Florian engaged enjoyably with various people, short conversations like musical chairs, but Antonella just smiled and fought with her inner self. She was obsessed with keeping an eye on Lawrence, sure he intended to pounce at any moment. Instead, after his initial spotting of her, he had made himself at home, circulating among the guests and stopping at various tables to sit down for a moment to sample food and chitchat. Several times he danced with pretty women—younger women—which annoyed Antonella. She felt he was doing that on purpose to make her jealous. Then, as the meal wore on, she began to feel miffed that he was ignoring her. It didn't seem right that he was having a good time like an eligible bachelor, when he had come to spoil her own good time.

Suddenly cheers and clapping broke out, because Natalie and Woody had gotten up and strolled hand in hand to the dance floor. Other dancers moved off to the sides to let the wedding couple dance alone to the special song the band played. The bride and groom were old and graceful as they danced—he so much taller than she—and many of the onlookers became misty-eyed. After a minute, Woody beckoned everyone to join them, and the band shifted to a lively, popular song. Florian smiled at Antonella and held out his hand. "Shall we, my love? I'm actually in the mood." Antonella nodded, and they crossed the lawn to the dance area. It was full of people, but they squeezed in near Woody and Natalie, who grinned and welcomed them. The dancing gave Antonella something to do besides dwelling on Lawrence. But when the next dance started, he was right there, and cut in on Woody. She heard Natalie's high-spirited laugh as her favorite of Antonella's lovers became her dance partner. "Oh, *dottore*, I was hoping you'd ask me to dance. You look so handsome tonight."

Woody cut in on Florian. "May I?"

"Just this once, and don't let her go to your head," Florian said facetiously.

"That'll be hard, but I'll do my best."

Florian moved off, and Antonella relaxed a bit, as if her problem had been momentarily postponed, even though Lawrence was dancing so close to her—at least Florian was out of his reach. And Woody was a good dancer, she had to pay attention to follow his quick steps.

Then she saw Florian dancing with Donatella and felt a pang of jealousy. He must have noticed her earlier and made a point of seeking her out once Woody cut in. Donatella was leaning back against Florian's hands around her waist in order to talk to him in her fast, animated way—as fluent in English as Italian. Her hands went up and down on his shoulders in rhythm to her speech. Florian wore an expression of total enchantment.

"Who's that woman?" Woody asked.

"Donatella—my sister-in-law—you've met her, Woody!"

"Why of course, but I didn't recognize her. You know, I've seen her mostly on TV."

Florian danced Donatella over to Antonella and Woody. "Double cut?" he said, debonairly.

Donatella and Antonella kissed. "Glad I had a chance to meet your sexy lover," Donatella said in Italian.

"What did she say?" Florian said.

"I said I was glad to meet Antonella's sexy lover," Donatella said in English.

"Oh, why thank you." He gave a little bow.

"And I'm glad to have this dance," Woody said with a gallant smile as he took possession of the black-wrapped body nearly as tall as he.

Florian and Antonella danced, and Florian raised his voice to be heard over the music, "What a fascinating woman! She said she did research at the Masters and Johnson Institute before it closed."

"She's a sex specialist."

"Yeah. I wonder what that's like—I mean, you must have to test out the full range of sexual behaviors in order to understand them and give advice to couples. And she also studied with shamans at a Carlos Castaneda center in Mexico."

"She's amazing, she's traveled the world for her work."

"But she spoke so fast, I missed half of the details. Maybe she'll come sit with us." He had no idea she was Lawrence's sister.

With alarm, Antonella saw Lawrence come up behind Florian and tap him on the shoulder. Florian was a head taller and stared at the stranger cutting in on him—someone too good-looking to leave alone with Antonella, someone who had obviously noticed her lack of a wedding ring. But, following etiquette, Florian tossed his head arrogantly and stepped aside so that Lawrence could move in and dance with Antonella.

Lawrence looked at her as he held out his hand and hers slipped into it. She thought he must have told the band what to play next, for it was starting up, and it was a song they both knew and had danced to many times before. It had a dreamy, sensual beat, and he moved her around to it with a light touch. It was like dancing in slow motion, as he wound her under his arm, and then pulled her back to him with a soft bump against his chest, his hand firm on her back. He kept a neutral expression, though his brown eyes were intent whenever they met hers. She thought how she had met him dancing at an August wedding seven years before, and now she was dancing with him again at another August wedding, this time with so much history between them. History is what accumulated with long-term couples.

When the song got to its high, amorous "ahh" notes, Antonella let herself go, entering the soulful music, feeling and remembering the sheer eroticism of dancing with Lawrence. It was like floating. She didn't have to pay attention the way she had with Woody. Lawrence directed everything as if she moved on air. And when her nose landed in the neck of his shirt, she smelled the skin that had always drawn her in like home. With closed eyes, she let herself succumb to his strength and his ease moving their bodies. She felt his hands that knew her contours by heart, making it effortless to wind her around and pull her against him, never missing a beat. As the song neared its end, he spun her and rocked her from behind, only for those fleeting seconds of the dance move, but in those seconds, with his head against her hair, she heard him say, "*Cosa vuoi?*" What do you want? When he brought her back around, his deep-set eyes looked once more into hers, as if repeating the words, "*Cosa vuoi?*"

The music slowly faded. They came apart. Then he thanked her with his half smile and moved off. But he had left his essence all over her, his warmth and soul, and she returned to her table feeling shaky and vulnerable.

Florian stared at her as she took her seat next to him. "Who was that dude with his hands all over you?"

"Lawrence."

"That's what I thought. Well, fuck him. He acted like you're still his wife."

"Technically I am."

He stared for a beat. "Did you know he was coming here?"

"Of course not."

"Nice send off for me."

He leaned back on two legs of his chair and folded his arms across his chest. "Well, the party's over for me with him here—let's go. This is my last night with you."

"Okay, in just a minute." But she couldn't imagine leaving with him. Something had happened, had changed, and they sat there in silence, pretending to watch the dancers.

Out of the blue, materializing from groups of people circulating around the table, Lawrence passed behind Florian's chair, and whatever he did with a sleight of hand, Florian's chair went down backwards. In the confusion that followed, Lawrence vanished, and only he and Antonella had witnessed his action.

Concerned guests immediately surrounded Florian who sat on the ground next to his chair, which one of the guests set upright. He was shaken and baffled at how he had lost his balance. Donatella was kneeling beside him, her dress up to her crotch. She had a comforting arm around his shoulder. "Are you all right? Do you need a doctor? My brother's here—I can go find him."

"I'm not hurt, just stunned."

"Of course you are. Try to relax, take deep breaths." She demonstrated.

Natalie and Woody arrived with water and helped Florian back to his feet and into his chair. "You'll be fine in a few minutes. And I hope you won't sue us for the bad chair," Woody said.

Antonella saw Lawrence on the deck opening the sliding doors to the clubhouse. She felt her heart beating strangely. With the flick of his hand he had toppled his rival—he, a doctor, who had taken an oath to "do no harm" and uphold medical ethics. He had deliberately harmed Florian. She forced herself to believe that he foresaw no serious consequences to the man landing on the grass, but still, how could he be sure?

No one noticed her slip away. All attention was centered on Florian, including his attention on himself. If anyone did see her, they assumed she was going to the ladies room. As she came up the steps to the deck, she saw Lawrence through the sliding doors, and he saw her, as if he had waited there for her. They watched each other as she came in, and he knew from her look that she came with her heart, however shaky. His right hand lifted, and she took it. Their hands squeezed and they smiled, tentatively. They would need time, but anger and remorse were gone. Life involved acceptance, of so many things—that was the feeling that passed between them.

Still holding hands, they left the party and headed down the driveway to the parking lot, their sides brushing familiarly, as if their innermost selves joined right there at the hip and hadn't been separated for more than a year. The night was all around them, Rome's ethereal beauty. When they reached his motorcycle, Lawrence murmured, *"Amore."*

Antonella closed her eyes and felt the word, the sound of his voice. She marveled that once again she was accepting the yoke of marriage, and with the same man. He might stray again, but so might she. But it didn't seem to matter. Something about the two of them, together, transcended the outer world. It wasn't passion that linked them, for passion didn't last. And it wasn't the kids. It was as if they shared a single core inside—two souls in one. Nothing could separate them down there at the strangely merged core, not even death. It was their cosmic connection. What a night it had been, Antonella thought—both she and Natalie reuniting with their soul partners.

With tenderness, Lawrence put on her helmet, smiling with his deep-set eyes as he snapped the buckle. Then he put on his own. She climbed onto the machine behind him, and he waited while she settled herself, taking his waist.

She loved the feel of his hard thighs balancing them, and he loved the feel of hers hugging his hips. He revved the engine a few times in preparation, and then, with smooth acceleration they took off into Rome's night, Rome's streets, Rome's imperial curves and breathing relics. The city and its ineffable eternity became a single pulse with them.